Belinda Hollyer grew up in New Zealand and
returns as often as possible. She lives most of
the time in London, where she has a cat-shaped
hole in her life, and some of the time in Key
West, Florida, where she shares a cat called
Minnie Mouser.

Secrets, Lies and My Sister Kate is her third
novel for Orchard.

ORCHARD BOOKS
338 Euston Road, London, NW1 3BH
Orchard Books Australia
Level 17/207 Kent Street, Sydney NSW 2000

ISBN 978 1 84616 690 7

1 3 5 7 9 10 8 6 4 2
Printed in the UK.

The paper and board used in this paperback are natural recyclable
products made from wood grown in sustainable forests.
The manufacturing processes conform to the environmental
regulations of the country of origin.

Orchard Books is a division of Hachette Children's Books,
an Hachette Livre UK company.
www.orchardbooks.co.uk

Secrets, LIES and my Sister Kate

Belinda Hollyer

ORCHARD BOOKS

1

Of all the things I mind about in my life, and the list is so long that if I wrote everything down it would stretch from here to Tierra del Fuego, which as you may know is an island at the bottom of South America, my own name is right at the top.

Mum and Dad don't get it, sometimes they even act surprised when I complain, although I don't see how surprise could enter into it.

Mum says, 'Oh darling, it's a lovely name, really unusual, and we thought you'd be happy with a name that no one else was likely to have. It's very distinctive, you know. I hope you'll grow into it, like the smell of coffee.'

I knew what she meant about coffee but I didn't admit that, because I was cross with her. The thing is that when I was little I used to hate the smell of coffee. I thought it was so horrible I'd go to the cupboard and open the packet and sniff it, just so I could check on how weird it was that grown-ups rolled their eyes with pleasure and said, 'Mmm! Coffee! Doesn't it smell great!' while I was thinking, 'Coffee! Yuck!

And then one day recently, I noticed that coffee had started to smell rather nice. I didn't want to drink it, I still don't, but it does seem that my sense of smell has changed, which is probably to do with growing up.

So Mum thinks that when I'm older, I will like my name.

How unlikely is that?

Very unlikely, I can tell you.

What I think is that hell could freeze over and the snows on Mount Kilimanjaro, which as you may know is a very high triple volcano in Tanzania, could melt away entirely, but I will still not like my name.

Dad ruffles my hair and says, 'Oh sweetie, what's the problem? I just call you Mini or Sweet Pea, anyway.' His face sort of softened when he said that, like he was going off somewhere in his mind, which in fact he was.

'I can still remember the moment I first saw you in the maternity ward,' he went on, 'curled up beside your mother like a little flower.'

I often find Dad embarrassing. Some of the things

he says and does go straight to the top of the list of things I mind about. They can even nudge my name out of what I think is called pole position – like when he wears his old red trousers in public, or dances to the music they play in supermarkets. But – and this is odd, because I wouldn't want him to say it in front of anyone outside our family – I have to admit it's nice to be remembered as a little flower.

It doesn't help my problem, though. I can't ask the rest of the world to call me Sweet Pea. Sweet Pea would be even worse in public than my real name. And I could also say, well, it's OK for you, Dad. His name's Peter and you can't get much more unexceptional than that.

But my sister Kate understands how I feel. She always does.

Kate says, 'You can change your name, you know, if it turns out that you *never* like it. When you're eighteen you can change it by Deed Poll and have a completely new name. There's all sorts of stuff you can do then.' And she added, 'It's going to be useful, being eighteen,' which at the time I thought she meant for me, although later on I realised she was actually talking to herself.

Anyway, changing my name sounds like a plan. It's just a pity I have to wait so long.

'What name *would* you like instead?' Kate asked

me the other day, when I was moaning on to her for the millionth time. 'Have you thought about choosing a different one?'

Well, duh! Of course I've thought about it. There's a girl in my class called Ruby, which is a name I like. Short and snappy but still a bit unusual, which I can see the point of. I wouldn't want a name that everyone else had, not that that's going to happen if I stay with the one I've got now. And I wouldn't like Ruby's name anyway, because she's trouble. If you don't like someone, it can put you off their name as well; probably for life. But still.

Last year two sisters from New York were at our school for a term. Madison was in my class and Taylor was the year above me. Madison told me that her name, which I admired until she told me this, had been chosen by her mother because she liked shopping on a street in New York City called Madison, which she said has the smartest shops anywhere in the world. The thing is, though, who wants to be named after a street? I think it should be the other way round: first you get famous and then you get a street named after *you*. And maybe that's true anyway, because Kate says that the Madison street, which is actually an avenue, was named after an American president. So it's from a president, to an avenue, to a girl with braces on her bottom teeth.

But what I do still like about Madison's name, and Taylor's too for that matter, is that you can't tell from it whether she's a boy or a girl. I think that's seriously cool, and I mentioned it to Kate.

Kate said, 'Like with Frances? It's all in the spelling. An 'e' for girls and an 'i' for boys.'

And we talked about that for a while, like Laurie in *Little Women* who's a boy although these days Laurie is a girls' name, and Lesley which is a spelling thing again; if it's a man it's Leslie, and Kate said that Joyce and Evelyn could be men's names too, although I have to say I seriously doubt that. Even Kate can make mistakes.

I'm still thinking about a name to choose when I'm eighteen. I'll probably start a list of possibles soon, so that I'll be ready when the time comes. Meantime, I asked Kate if *she* still minds about her name, too, which she used to do, although not as much as me. But these days, she says she doesn't. She doesn't even mind any more that Dad calls her Maxi, like he calls me Mini, although she used to hate that. I remember when she'd refuse to answer Dad when he called her Maxi, which is a technique that works like a charm, but only if you keep your resolve. I'm not that good at resolve, I give in too soon and sometimes I even forget what the resolve was

9

supposed to be all about.

'Kate's not my real name and neither's Maxi, so it's like I have a secret name,' she explained.

Kate's more into secrets than me, but this may be something I will grow into, like with the coffee.

Kate's real name, the one on her birth certificate, is Katerina. In fact, her whole name is Katerina Gwendolyn Minor. And you might think that's bad but I can assure you that mine is a lot worse.

Parents can be very cruel. They may not mean to be, but it happens anyway. Like when they fight, which our parents do a lot more than I think they should. We all have strong opinions in our house, so when we clash it's rather noisy. But when Mum and Dad argue they take noisy to a whole other level. It's no fun when they're shouting at each other, I can tell you. Afterwards, when they've made up, they say things like, '*Oh Mini darling, we don't mean anything, it's just our way,*' but I hate it anyway.

Kate doesn't like it either, but she has the knack of not seeming to mind as much as me. She can switch off and pretend it's not happening, it's almost like she can flip a switch in her head so the yelling and tears and door slamming don't get through to her. It's like her silent resolve about not answering to a name she doesn't like; it shows the determination in her character.

I can't do that. I wish I could.

On the plus side, which is how Kate puts it, the way Mum and Dad fight has made the two of us closer than we might have been otherwise, what with the gap in our ages. Kate is three years and five months older than me, which is a lot for a best friend. When we are in our thirties, say, which is a weird thing to imagine because it's so far away, that amount of difference probably won't be important. Some of Mum's friends are years younger or older than her, and it never seems to matter to any of them. But when you are growing up, which is where we are right now, it does. So we might not have got on so well if everything at home was sweetness and light. Kate has always looked after me when things get difficult.

My earliest memory is being out in the back garden at night with Kate, without knowing how we got there. Kate was holding my hand, and listening to shouting inside the house. She must have put on our dressing gowns and picked up some socks from the washing pile as we went through the house, so we could warm our feet up while we waited. I don't remember being cold, only confused, but I knew I was safe because Kate was there too. She sat me down on the grass and gave me a sock at a time, and helped me to pull them up when they stuck. Kate put on the other socks herself, and I remember giggling because they didn't match, and anyway they were inside out.

'They're not even yours!' I shouted, forgetting that we were hiding, and Kate shushed me with her head on one side, still listening. The shouting had stopped.

'I think they've stopped arguing now' she said, finally. 'We can go back to bed.'

But in my memory we didn't go inside right away. Instead, we sat holding hands on the grass with our dressing gowns bunched under our legs, and then Kate put her arm around me and told me a story about a mouse who'd lost his way home.

I think that's where our travel game began, with the mouse story. We used to play it all the time when we were younger, and we still do it a lot – well I do anyway, and Kate joins in if I tell her where I'm going and how far I've got. She doesn't start it off much any more, though.

The travel game is a kind of secret between us, although it's not like we hide away to play it, or pretend that we're not when we are. And Mum and Dad know about it, although they don't get the real point. They get that I'm a Geography Star, so I always do the navigating when we go anywhere in the car. And when we watch a quiz show on TV, if there's a geography question, they always look at me to see if I know the answer. But it's like they think the travel game's just about naming Capital Cities of Europe, or Rivers of the World, or knowing how to get to the motorway quickly, which it isn't.

Dad says that my geography thing must be the result of having extra iron in my nose. I'm not sure if he's joking or not. He probably is. He claims that's how migrating birds find magnetic north and navigate their way across oceans, by having iron deposits in their beaks. He says people have iron in their noses for the same reason, and he reckons I've got more than other people.

It all sounds like a typical Dad joke, but I think he's slightly serious about it because he did an experiment once where he blindfolded me and spun me round on the whirly desk chair in the den, and then asked me to point north. It could have been a fluke, me getting it right every time, and I'm not doing it for him again because it's like being a performing dog. And anyway, that's nothing to do with why I'm good at geography.

I'm not saying I don't like getting geography things for presents, particularly if they're about earthquakes or volcanoes, which I am most interested in at the moment. I have already put in a request for a particular volcano book for my next birthday, which is only five weeks and three days away from now.

But I mostly like geography because, if you know about other places in the world, you can go there in your imagination whenever you want. And doing that can be a whole lot more fun than staying where you are in real life. Like me and Kate, right at this exact moment, sprawled side by side on her bed staring up at the ceiling, waiting for Mum to come home so we can go shopping with her.

Going shopping with Mum is close to the top of my list of things I don't like about my life, but what can you do when your mother insists you help her with something? In my case, *feel resentful* is the answer. In Kate's case, though, it's more often, *solve the problem*, and you have to admire her for that. Waiting around was getting on her nerves too, but instead of getting cross like I was doing she just glanced at me and said, 'Where did we get to last time, Mini?' And immediately my crossness smoothed out and vanished like it had never existed.

'Tashkent,' I said, closing my eyes. 'We were watching the silk weavers.'

Tashkent's a city in Central Asia and the name means The Stone Fortress. In ancient times it had a different name – Ming Uruk – which means The Thousand Apricot Orchard. I used to imagine that I lived in Tashkent, in a little flat-roofed house with a garden filled with apricot trees. But when I told Kate about that she suggested we should do a trip from Tashkent, because it's on an old travel route called the Silk Road, and caravans carrying silk all the way from China to Europe used to travel through Tashkent. (That's caravans of pack camels loaded up with stuff, not the sort of caravan you tow behind cars, by the way, which I didn't realise until Kate told me, years ago.) We've made lots of journeys around Tashkent now: it's a real favourite of ours. We've never gone the whole way along the Silk Road, though; we only do little bits of it.

'What colour silk are you choosing for your pack?' asked Kate. 'I'm having the purple,' she added quickly, but that was OK because I already knew I wanted apricot coloured silk, which would remind me of Tashkent's apricot trees all the way to Samarkand, which is the next stop on the western road. It isn't far away, only about 150 kilometres, but we're on camels so it takes a couple of days.

'I'm going to wear mine,' said Kate, sounding thoughtful. 'Well, some of it, anyway. Wrapped around my head like a turban.'

Purple will suit her, with her dark hair and pale skin. I don't know why she doesn't wear it ordinarily, except that these days she goes for black almost all the time, which also looks good on her. She's got what Mum calls *arresting colouring*. I thought that meant she was going to be put in jail, the first time Mum said it, but it's just another word for stunning. If I didn't love Kate, if she wasn't my best friend ever as well as my sister, I'd probably be jealous of how she looks. But right now I just wanted to get on.

'Look, Kate,' I said, 'I reckon the silk's ready for us now. Let's load up our packs and choose our camels. The stables are just down the street.'

I love choosing the camels. A lot of why I've stuck with the Silk Route for so long is because of the camels. Sometimes I choose a camel to ride that has a baby and then the baby comes too, pacing along beside its mother or gambolling off to the side and having its own adventures. And choosing camels is how we collect the first points in the game. But Kate and I had only just started walking towards the camel stables when the front door slammed downstairs.

It had to be Mum.

I opened my eyes and looked over at Kate, and pulled a face. She grinned at me with her mouth turned down at the corners, which is her way of signalling, *Well, but what can you do?*

Mum called out that she was back, and could we

16

please hurry up or we'd run out of time.

Talk about a spoilsport.

Shopping with Mum is the very opposite of choosing silk or camels with Kate. It's all hurry hurry, and having to make up your mind in Mum's time, which takes her a millisecond, and not in mine, which takes a bit longer.

I admit that Mum doesn't have much free time, and I know she likes to be super-efficient and have everything timetabled and organised and happening exactly when it's supposed to. But still. We help her when we can and I've even offered to help by *not* going shopping at all, which would surely save everyone aggravation, but that isn't an option as far as Mum's concerned. We have to do it together, all three of us, with a running commentary from Mum, which in itself is enough to drive you crazy.

Mum runs a bakery from home. She makes little cupcakes, except that hers are square instead of round like most cupcakes. If you stop to think about it, her square ones aren't actually cupcakes at all, because who would want a square cup? But that's still what they're called.

Mum started by making just a few and selling them to a local coffee shop, but now her cakes are dead fashionable and she sells them everywhere – to fancy department stores and even fancier grocery shops – and so she has to make hundreds of them every day. And then she spreads them with icing in different flavours, and you have to get the icing completely even all over the cakes or Mum can't sell them. And then she has to sprinkle sprinkles on them, all different kinds of sprinkles depending on where the cakes are going, and you have to do just the right amount of sprinkles or the shop phones her up to complain there aren't enough, and she has to rush in and add more on the spot. And she has to deliver them in special boxes to stop the cakes getting messed up in the back of her car.

One of Mum's friends helps her part-time, but still, it's a lot of work. And since it means we always have cakes to eat – because we get the ones that have gone wonky in the oven, or any that have broken or burned or are otherwise less than absolutely perfect – I probably shouldn't complain about how she rushes through the other things in her life. But it's hard not to, especially for me, because I am an ace complainer. Complaining comes naturally to me, almost before anything else.

But as it turned out, that afternoon's shopping was a whole lot better than I'd expected. At first we got so loaded down with bags and parcels that I felt resentfulness rising in my heart again. But then Kate started walking in front of me like a camel, kind of swaying smoothly along and taking big stiff steps, so I joined in behind her, like we were two pack camels in a caravan. Mum knew something was going on but not exactly what, and she got ratty, but we kept it up all through the supermarket and a special grocery shop and two department stores. At one point I felt inspired to be a baby camel and gallop off across the sand dunes, but I stumbled into a shopping trolley and almost fell over with all the shopping bags. So after that we just stayed in line, putting our heads in the air and moaning quietly through our noses the way camels do. I know it was crazy but it made the time pass very quickly, even though we kept getting the giggles and turning the moaning noises into snorting laughter, and in the end Mum slightly lost it and started hissing at us, *'Behave! You're in public!'* Which just made me do the camel moan slightly louder.

I can see it could be annoying to have a child like me, which is what Mum ends up saying when she becomes totally exasperated. On the other hand, from my point of view, it's annoying to have to go shopping, and you have to do something to cheer yourself up.

2

When we got back home Dad was there and in a good mood, so Mum cheered up and got us busy making dinner together. She'd bought wonton wrappers in the Asian food shop, and you're supposed to wrap them around a filling to make little parcels, and then cook them in soup like dumplings. But Mum wanted to try making Italian-style ravioli – little pasta parcels – with them instead. Kate chopped up spinach for the filling, and Dad and I formed a production line adding cheese and herbs to the spinach, and Mum did the final wrapping and the cooking. The results were truly excellent. There are advantages to having a good cook for a mother.

And another good thing was, Kate and I got back to the Silk Road later on. Kate had planned to hang out with a couple of her friends after dinner but it didn't happen, and Mum wanted to watch a cooking programme on TV so she'd taken over the comfy sofa in the living room, and Dad was on the computer in the den, fiddling around on a new website he'd found. You know how it is when you first discover something fun, and you can't think about anything else? Dad's like that with the Internet right now; you'd think he'd invented it. Kate says we'll just have to wait for him to get over it, and then *we* can get back on the computer.

So anyway, after we'd stacked the dishwasher, the two of us went up to her room. Kate's room is better than mine. I don't mind that, but it's a fact. Partly it's better because it's bigger, but the main reason is it's right at the very top of the house so it has sloping ceilings and you see sky and the tops of trees through the skylight windows, which is inspirational. When you lie on her bed you can watch clouds scudding or floating along, and go into quite a dreamy state.

You can't see much sky at night, of course. You can't see any stars, for example, because the streetlights are too bright. But it's still good to have that view, and Kate never pulls the blinds down, even in summer. She doesn't mind being woken early with the light; in fact she likes it. And she's done up the room with posters and pictures, and collections of things arranged on the shelves. She has miniature china cats, and interesting pebbles, and she's just started a new collection of tiny feathers.

She's also got an embroidered rug on the floor that she found in a skip and dragged home. Mum wanted to get it cleaned before Kate used it because she thought there might be bugs or worse in it, though you might wonder, what could be worse than bugs? In the end, Kate and I just washed it in the bath with disinfectant in the water. The colours ran into each other but that made it look even better. Kate calls it her camel rug and she uses it at night to keep the baby camels warm. It does get cold at night along the desert road, although personally I think the baby camels' thick fur would keep them cosy, or they could cuddle up to their mothers. But Kate has a very soft heart.

We spent ages at the camel stables that night, choosing teams of camels for our caravan. We've never been sure what sort of camels live in Tashkent – whether it's the ones with two humps, or the sort with only one. Kate says the two-hump ones have sweeter natures and are less likely to bite you, which one-hump camels are very prone to do. You get more points for choosing one-hump camels because of that, but it evens out because you lose points for baby camels and we both want to have them too. In the end we hedged our bets as usual and chose some of each kind of camel, and some with babies. Then we lined them all up and decided which ones would carry the bales of silk, and the tents, and the food. And us, of course.

It was dark when we finally set off across the plains, but that was OK because the stars are so bright you can see where you're going without artificial light. I haven't learned how to navigate a journey by the stars – not in ordinary life; not yet. I can do grid references on maps and I know about latitude and longitude, but so far that's it. In the game, though, I use the stars to find my way like travellers did hundreds of years ago. But the truth is that we've made the journey so often, and we know where we're going without having to use stars, or maps, or even a compass.

It was a school night, so I had to go to bed sooner than I wanted; I'd rather have stayed on the journey and got as far as the oasis, which was going to be our first stop. I like settling the camels down at the oasis, and giving them nosebags to eat from, and then rolling myself up in a sleeping bag by the campfire.

While I was getting into bed I thought of a way to liven things up the next time we played. A gang of fierce marauders could attack us while we were sleeping, and the points would depend on how we managed to fight them off. I like to introduce surprises because I want to keep Kate interested in the game.

I wanted to decide which way the marauders would come before I put out my light. My room is smaller than Kate's, with an ordinary window rather than skylights, which is another reason why hers is better than mine. But my room has one great advantage: it is *completely* covered with maps! Every centimetre of the walls, and even most of the ceiling, has maps stuck to it instead of wallpaper.

Dad works in a place that buys and sells office equipment, and last year they got a huge box of old maps. No one else wanted them; everyone said they were junk, but Dad knew better so he brought them home. And then he papered my bedroom walls and ceiling with them, just like wallpaper. Well, not *exactly* like wallpaper, in actual fact, because a lot of the maps were torn, and some were just bits of maps and not the whole thing. He had to stick them like patchwork, all layered on top of each other. Higgledy-piggledy, Mum called it.

Some of the maps have writing in foreign languages and I don't have a clue what they show. Some of them have little numbers instead of words; I think those ones are sea charts. So mostly you have to use your imagination on them, which is just the sort of challenge I like to have.

And when I thought of the marauders on the desert road, I looked at the map in the corner by my wardrobe that has mountain ranges. I decided the marauders had a mountain hideout and a stable full of racing camels, so they could come sweeping down into our valley. And I went to sleep happy because, of course, I had already worked out how to beat off the attack.

The next morning, though, I remembered something I'd completely forgotten the night before, about school.

A new boy arrived in our class last week, and Mr Simpson put him in the seat beside me. 'For the present,' is what Mr Simpson said, and I thought of answering him with that old joke about, 'So OK, where's my present, then?' But I didn't. I like Mr Simpson, and a lot of Bart Simpson jokes come his way so he's more or less joked out. And another reason not to say it is because no one likes a smarty-pants, which Kate tells me that I tend to be, especially when I've got up her nose, which does occasionally happen. I see that I can be hard work at times, though I don't think that's necessarily such a bad thing. I might not think that if I wasn't me, though.

But there's a third good reason to be careful

around Mr Simpson, and this is it.

Mr Simpson almost certainly knows what my real name is, although he always calls me Mini because I asked him to. I ask every teacher to do that; I always have, since I started school. And if he went off me he might reveal my true name to the whole class, and then I'd die of embarrassment, or if I didn't die I'd absolutely have to run away. So I need to keep him sweet.

Mr Simpson probably put this new boy next to me because he knows I don't mind sitting next to a boy. Lots of people in my class would hate having to sit next to a MOOS, which is what most of our year call a Member Of the Opposite Sex. They say it like moose and roll their eyes like it's a terrible thing. Like having bubonic plague. Or living on the slopes of Mauna Loa, which is in Hawaii and is the world's largest active volcano, and if you were the nervous type you'd find that a worrying place to spend time.

But my first proper friend at school, way back in Year One, was a boy – Joe. We would have been friends for longer, I think, but his family moved to Japan.

On the subject of friends, I might as well admit that I don't tend to have many. Not close friends, anyway. At school they mostly think I'm weird because of the geography thing – either that, or they think I'm boring because I'm so interested in it. I have learned the hard way not to share interesting geographical facts in public.

And if I do find a friend who doesn't mind me going on about things like pyroclastic debris – which in case you want to know are the fragments of volcanic material that are blown out in an explosion – well, they tend to move away, like Joe did. Which is a pain, and another complaint about my life, although I don't take it personally. I mean, I don't think Joe's family moved because of me – I'm not *that* weird. But the thing is, Joe set a standard of OK-ness for boys as friends so I don't object to them the way some girls do.

Anyway. The new boy's name is Satch, which interests me because that *has* to be a nickname, doesn't it? No one could possibly be called Satch right from the start, could they? It wouldn't go on your birth certificate.

There's no chance that his real name's as dire as mine. But medium-dire, there's certainly a chance of it.

Satch is tall and thin and very pale, with glasses. Those first three things could easily have got him a nickname like Spaghetti, and adding Four Eyes for the glasses could be even more depressing. For all I know, Spaghetti Four Eyes is what he was called at his last school, which could have been a good reason to leave. But he doesn't come across like someone you should feel sorry for, so I don't intend to. I did budge over for him, and I helped him in the first few lessons, too. I showed him the books he needed, and where the science lab was – that sort of thing. But it's just politeness, not charity.

I'd like to ask him about his name if I get to know him better. Not that it's likely to happen any time soon because he didn't say *one single word* all yesterday! It seems weird, especially since I was noticeably helpful to him and that would normally get a few words out of a new person.

So far he's only grunted. He grunted a yes, and later on there was a slightly different grunt for thanks, when I lent him my red pen. I knew what he meant both times. But there wasn't one actual word out of him.

For a while I wondered if he even spoke English. But he must do, he reads and writes in it. It can't be that, Mr Simpson would have said.

And what I'd forgotten was my plan to get to know Satch better. What I have done in the past, and it always works, is take some of Mum's leftover cakes to school. Sometimes I do that even when I don't have anything to gain because no one minds cupcakes that are slightly crooked or crumbled, or a bit burned at the edges. It's not exactly a way to make friends, but it is a way to keep people off my back. And if I give some to Satch he'll *have* to say thank you, and we could get talking, and then I could ask him about his name.

But I forgot to ask Mum to save rejects for me. She bakes cakes late at night or early in the morning, and sometimes she throws out the rejects before we can get them. Mum thinks we eat too much cake as it is, and that we shouldn't have sweet things every single day. I disagree with that. I think you should seize your opportunities with both hands, and that definitely includes Mum's cupcake rejects.

Mum turned our basement into a bakery last year, when her cake business expanded. She stopped using our ordinary kitchen because there wasn't enough room to spread out the trays or store the cakes while they cooled. Now she's got a restaurant-type setup down there, so if there were any rejects still around that's where they'd be.

Well, the rejects were there, and so was Dad. He was sitting with a huge cup of coffee and a big plate of cakes, and he looked slightly guilty when I appeared. I knew why, of course. Mum is keen on us all eating healthy food, which is slightly ironic from someone who sells iced cakes for a living, but there you go.

So, cake *first thing in the morning?* For *breakfast?* Mum would go mad; she'd bang on about vitamins and minerals for hours if she knew. But she'd already left to make deliveries, which was how Dad had managed to sneak down for an early morning sugar fix.

I pulled up another stool and dragged the plate of cakes over for a quick look. There were plenty for me to take into school *and* eat a couple now, as long as I could stop Dad from motoring through too many more, so I put another two on a plate to keep him happy, and chose two for myself. Both of mine had a lot of crust dripping down the sides, just like the lava in a central vent volcanic eruption, and as it happens that's exactly how I like my cupcakes. And they were still very warm; Mum must have baked early that morning. I finished the first one, licked my lips, and started on the second.

'You're early this morning, Mini,' said Dad through a mouthful.

I explained why I'd come down; I thought that telling him about my plan might keep him away from the rest of the cakes. And when I said about Satch, Dad pushed his plate away with a smile.

'I'm off now, and I've had my fill anyway,' he said, patting his tummy. 'Got to watch my waistline.'

I raised my eyebrows in mock disbelief: Dad's one

of those people who never puts on weight, no matter how much he eats. Kate's like that too; I expect she gets it from him.

Thinking of Kate made me wonder if she'd like some too. It wouldn't matter – Mum must have rejected just about a whole tray from the last baking. I ran upstairs to Kate's room.

'Have you had breakfast yet?' I asked her. 'Because I'm taking a few of Mum's rejects to school, but you could have some too if you want. There are lots left.'

Kate grinned at me. She looked like she always does, which is totally terrific. This morning she'd swept her hair up into a sort of a bun on the side of her head with little bits coming down over her face. On anyone else it might look stupid but on Kate it's like the latest fab fashion statement – like *everyone* should be wearing their hair that way.

'Thank you, Sweet Pea!' she said, teasing me. She knows I don't mind that nickname so she sometimes uses it as well as Dad.

'I don't want them for me,' she added, 'but I'll take a couple into school if you can spare them. Are you sure?'

I nodded.

'My year group is filled with hungry boys,' Kate went on. She wrinkled her nose when she said that, to show that the idea of boys, especially hungry ones, wasn't an attractive one for her. But I thought I knew better. Kate's friend Lee has an older brother called Johnny, and I'm pretty sure that Kate fancies him. He's not in her year, he's in Year Eleven where frankly they're all a bit scary, but Kate says Johnny's OK when you get to know him. I expect she thinks Mum's cakes could help her get to know him better.

I wanted to mention my plan about Satch, because I thought she might admit to having a plan about Johnny if I did. But there wasn't enough time to explain it so we ran down to the basement together and discovered that Dad had left his second cake untouched on his plate, which was good. Kate only wanted two cakes anyway, and that left five for me to use on Satch.

And then, even though there was hardly any time left, Kate suddenly decided to clean up the cake trays for Mum. It drives me mad when people rush things at the last moment and the only thing about Kate that gets to me is how she'll go for a last minute extra delay, when there's hardly enough time left for what you're already doing. I didn't argue, though, because I know she was trying to help Mum. Sometimes Kate and Mum don't get along very well, and then one or the other of them does something extra nice to make up. Anyway, it's Kate's business if she misses her bus and gets a detention for being late.

I went up to the kitchen for a lunchbox while she was still faffing around, putting things away in cupboards and fiddling with the utensil drawer that always sticks, because Mum tends to shove her paperwork in behind the measuring spoons and beaters. It took Kate ages, and when she came upstairs she looked all hot and bothered. Like – well, like she had something unexpected on her mind.

Madison used to say, when someone in our year was upset, *'You look like you lost a dollar and found a dime!'* But Kate looked more like she'd lost a dollar and found a nasty surprise instead.

And what was extra weird, was this. She shoved an envelope into her backpack, but it fell out again and hit the floor with a sort of slithery clunk. Paper doesn't clunk so there must have been something heavy inside the envelope. I wondered what it was and looked over, but Kate just swore under her breath and grabbed it again, and she didn't even say goodbye properly to me before she left.

Looking back, I can see that's when all the trouble started – when Kate was downstairs, trying to be The Good Daughter.

3

As it turned out I was even later leaving than Kate, so I only just caught my bus. I was a bit bothered about what had just happened. I know Kate so well – better than I know even myself – so I can tell if something's wrong. But then I forgot about it in the excitement of putting The Cupcake Plan into action.

The bus got me to school about fifteen minutes before register, which was perfect. And when I got to our classroom Satch was already at his desk, next to mine. Also perfect. There were other people around, but they seemed too busy with their own things to interfere. So I walked over with the cupcake box in my hand, and held it out to Satch.

He looked at the box, and then at me. Then he sort of *looked* a question instead of asking it in words. He didn't say, '*Well, duh, what's this about?*' But he raised his eyebrows and looked surprised.

Not in an unfriendly way, though. Just being silent, like before.

I didn't say anything; I just kept holding the box out in silence. It was a see-through plastic one so he could tell there was food in it, and I shook it a bit to make the offer more inviting.

Result! Satch took it and opened the lid, and peered in. The cakes were still slightly warm so you could smell how delicious they were. He picked one up and tasted it, and I could tell he really liked it because he took another one. I wasn't surprised: everyone loves Mum's cakes. In fact, a couple of boys who'd eaten them before were looking over. They'd be asking for a cake any minute, so I wanted to finish my plan quickly. I didn't lose my nerve, though. I just hung on, and I *still* didn't say anything to Satch.

Because my plan was to wait him out. In the end, how could he *not* say thank you for the cakes?

And I was right.

'Your cakes are very good,' he finally said through a mouthful of the second one. And OK, the cake muffled his voice but it sounded normal, which eliminated one reason I'd thought of for his silence. If his voice had been squeaky high, or if it had broken halfway through a word, that could have been enough to keep him quiet.

'Have some more,' I suggested. 'Finish them, why don't you? I brought them in for you. Mum makes them for her business, and these are leftovers.'

He took another one.

'Why for me?' he asked, before he put it in his mouth.

'Because you didn't say anything yesterday,' I explained. Satch looked surprised, but he took the last two cakes anyway.

'I knew you'd have to say thank you for them,' I went on. 'Then I'd find out if you had a voice.'

He grinned. Satch has a great smile, and that's when I first saw it in action. It lights up his whole face. You stop noticing how tall and skinny he is, and how big his glasses are; you only see the smile.

'Good plan, Mini,' he said. 'Good as your Mum's cakes.'

I waited again. I normally rush right into things, it's just my nature, and there wasn't much time before the bell so I was under pressure. But now I knew for sure that the waiting technique was successful, so I stuck with it.

It worked again.

'I don't say much,' Satch went on. 'Not at first.'

'Because?' OK, so I couldn't wait *forever*.

'I stammer,' he said carefully. 'Saying things can be tricky.'

I should have guessed. I might even have worked it out if I'd given myself more time. It was always going to be something like that, when I thought about it afterwards. And stammering's something I've met before, so I could definitely have thought of it as an option. One of Kate's friends still stammers when she's tired, and Kate says she – it's Lee in fact, the one with the brother – used to do it much, much worse. Like, *all the time*.

'So you'd rather not talk until you have to?' I asked Satch.

He nodded.

'Until I know how people will be about it.'

'You mean, like teasing?' I wasn't really asking a question; I was more making a statement, because I knew about that as well. Kate told me how Lee had been tormented through a whole school year. But Satch answered me anyway.

'Not just that. It's because people won't wait until I can get out whatever I'm trying to say. They get impatient or bored, and try to guess the words or finish my sentences for me. I hate that.'

'Worse than teasing?'

'Oh yeah,' said Satch. 'Teasing's something I hardly notice any more. It doesn't bother me as much as when they butt in.'

I thought about that while I put the empty box

37

away and got out what I needed for the first class. I knew Lee got stuck on T sounds so she'd try to avoid words that started with a T, which is actually a whole lot harder than you might think. But Satch didn't seem to have a special problem with T words – he didn't seem to have a problem with *any* words. He hadn't stammered once, yet.

We ended up on the same lunch table that day, so I asked him more about it then, and he said that stammering's not the same for everyone. T has never been a big deal for him; it was letters like B that get him into trouble. But not even all the time – sometimes he can't say a B at the start of a word without getting stuck on it, and other days that word's OK again. But new experiences – like arriving at our school – often made it start up big time, which was why he hadn't wanted to say anything at all the first day, if he could avoid it.

'Sometimes,' he said, 'when I think I'm going to have trouble saying stuff, I distract myself and make lists in my head. Playlists on my iPod, favourite movies, that kind of thing. It calms me down, so I can get past the problem.'

'It doesn't calm the people I'm talking to, though,' he added, grinning. 'They see my lips moving while I'm making a list but there's nothing coming out of my mouth. Or they see my fingers tapping to the music in my head as I'm counting up tracks, and man! They think, *"Weirdo! Geeky weirdo!"* and inch very slowly away from me.'

I didn't ask him about his name that day, but I think we might actually turn out to be friends, me and Satch. And if we do, I can ask him then.

My last good friend – apart from Kate who's always been my very best friend – left a year ago, and I haven't wanted to get close to anyone else in my class for obvious reasons. Obvious to me, anyway. There's the problem about everyone at school knowing me already and so they have a view about me being the Geography Star, and I can tell you, the opinions are not what you might call flattering. Not everyone is in-my-face mean about it, but it does put people off.

It's not a good idea to be different at school. Satch must also know that the hard way, because it's bad enough to be so tall and skinny if no one else is. When you're our age you'd rather blend in with other people if you can. A couple of girls in our class, Ruby and her best friend Jay, have already started calling him silly names. Today it was Spaghetti-O. He doesn't seem to mind, he just grins patiently and doesn't answer them. So it's probably true what he said about not caring if he's teased.

This idea of his, where you make lists in your

head, it's an interesting one. It's a bit like what Kate does when Mum and Dad argue: she sort of cuts out while it's happening, like she's switched off the audio channel. I don't see myself doing that, but the first chance I get I'll think up an interesting list. Like – well, for instance, like the names of ten places along the Silk Route. Or the names of ten of the volcanoes of the Pacific Ring of Fire, which as you may know is a ring of volcanoes and earthquake zones around the edge of the Pacific Ocean. If those don't distract me, I don't know what would.

I'm not going to rush Satch into being my friend, though. If we're going to be that's fine, but I don't want him to feel I'm too keen. I often jump into things before I've thought about them, so when they don't work I have only myself to blame.

I didn't think about Kate again until I was on my way home, by which time I decided I'd probably imagined how she'd seemed that morning. I thought she'd be back before me, anyway, and I could talk to her and see if she was OK. I expected she'd be more or less on time because she hadn't written anything down for after school.

Mum has a wall planner where we all write down when we'll be late home and where we'll be, with contact numbers and everything. Mum and Dad fill it in too which Kate says is the only way to keep track of our yo-yo parents. I know what she means; they do whirl around and in and out, all the time.

Mum isn't generally around first thing in the morning because of her cake deliveries, so Dad sees that we get off to school with everything we need. He even used to check our homework and he still sometimes makes us packed lunches. He's good at them. When Dad makes my lunch I know without checking that I'll like it, and have things to swap if I want to. His cheese and walnut sandwiches are very popular with my year.

But because she isn't around in the mornings, Mum always tries to be home when we get back from school. Kate's school is further away than mine, and we both have things to do afterwards, so we're often back at different times. But Mum's waiting for us, and ready to chat.

Mum thought Kate would be back on time, too. After the first hour went by and no Kate, Mum wondered if she'd forgotten to put down her new dance class, but I thought it was probably the bus. If she'd missed her usual one she'd have to wait around for ages, which had happened before.

I didn't think it was anything to worry about because I had absolutely no idea what Kate had on her mind. I can tell you, it was a shock to me when

I found out. It was probably the first time, ever, that I hadn't known what she was thinking about.

After another hour Mum started to worry so she tried Kate's mobile, but it was on voice mail. She phoned a couple of Kate's friends but they hadn't seen Kate since classes finished and didn't know where she was. So Mum got more anxious and phoned Dad at work, and asked him to come home. By the time he got back Kate *still* hadn't appeared.

She was almost three hours late by then. Even I thought it was strange, and Mum was totally spinning herself in a state. She said they should call the police then and there, but Dad persuaded her they should wait.

'There'll be an explanation,' he said. 'Kate's a big girl and she's sensible, too. Don't worry about it.'

I knew that wouldn't stop Mum worrying, and I could see they were heading for a row about it. Frankly I would rather have just worried about Kate all by myself than stuck around for one of their arguments. I hate it when they fight. And I was so busy hating the idea, as well as wondering about Kate, that I completely forgot to make a list in my head to distract myself. Honestly! I was cross about that as well, when I finally remembered.

If you actually listen, you can see a pattern to their arguments. First, Mum starts up about how she can't do everything in the home, and why doesn't Dad do more, and that he should shoulder more of the burden.

I resent her saying that. I don't see myself as a burden at all, even when I'm being difficult. And I wasn't.

Then Dad defends himself. He goes on about how he does everything he can, and how he has to be at work earning money to pay for it all, and why does she always get at him?

Pretty soon their voices rise and the 'You always...' and 'You never...' sentences get louder and louder. Mum has a hot temper so she often starts it but Dad always argues back, and once he's off he's like a dog with a bone, he'll never give up.

Listening to them winding themselves up makes me think of watching a grumbling volcano that's getting ready to blow. There's one on an island in the Indian Ocean, called Mount Karthala, which behaves like that. You get a red glimmer in the sky to start with, and the smell of burning earth, and then the ground starts to shake. After that, the lava erupts.

The thing is, they both get so stirred up they forget what caused the row in the first place, and go shouting off down another track entirely. Like how one of them behaved on a holiday they had three years ago, or even about how someone (Dad, usually) leaves the bathroom in a mess or someone (Mum, usually) doesn't put the dishtowel back on the rack. And if something doesn't stop them or distract them it usually ends with one of them slamming out of the room, or even out of the house altogether.

Well, to be fair, it doesn't actually end there because they do make up again. Sometimes on the spot, and sometimes the next day. And they usually say sorry to us as well. But Kate has the knack of finding a way to derail them or calm them down, so it was ironic that this one was all about *her* not being there. I sat in the corner thinking, *Where are you when we need you, Kate?*

And right when I was at the peak of wishing she was there, Kate walked in the door. Almost three and a half hours late.

There was a moment of complete silence when she came in. She acted like there was nothing wrong, she just said hello in a normal voice, dumped her backpack on the hall floor as usual, and wriggled out of her jacket. You have to hand it to her; she can keep her nerve.

The silence didn't last, of course. Mum pounced first, and then Dad joined in, and I just sat waiting for them to stop shouting and give Kate a chance to explain, and wondering what she'd say when they let her speak.

I didn't imagine it was anything serious. She was acting so normal I couldn't believe she had any big dramatic thing to reveal to the world.

And I still don't think so.

It's only a tattoo, for pity's sake. A really little one. No one will even see it or know it's there unless she wants them to. Mum really didn't need to burst into floods of tears when Kate admitted what she'd done, and rolled up her cardigan to show us the top of her arm.

In fact, Mum got even *more* upset when she finally saw it. She gave a sort of gasp and went white, and put her hand up to her throat. She even said *'A butterfly!'* in a quivery sort of voice.

What's wrong with a butterfly? It might have been a skull and cross bones, Mum.

Anyway, I don't think a tiny little tattoo is such a problem. Kate's arm is a bit red and puffy, but she says it will calm down and be OK in a day or two.

I'm not saying I want a tattoo, because I don't. At least I don't think so, not unless the whole subject turns out like the smell of coffee, in which case I might change my mind in a year or two. But Kate's tattoo is just a sweet little butterfly perched on her shoulder, and it's not much bigger than my little finger. It isn't enough of anything to make such a fuss about.

So after she'd confessed to having it done, and shown it off, and pointed out that she'd paid for it with her own money that she'd earned in her last holiday job, I thought we could all calm down and have our dinner.

Boy, was I wrong! The arguments went back and forth for ages more and then Mum said she didn't want dinner anyway, she was too upset to be hungry. I could see what she meant, because I had lost my appetite by the time Dad sat down with me and Kate, and I can tell you, that's very unusual.

So all round, it wasn't a good evening. But the strange thing was, I could actually see it from *their* point of view as well as from Kate's, which might actually be a first in my life.

Not about the tattoo. I thought they were being unreasonable about that. It's not life and death, and it is her shoulder, after all.

But I do see why they'd mind about Kate being home late and not saying she was going to be, which seems weird to me as well as cruel. She'd have known they'd be worried if she'd thought about it at all.

I didn't want to tell Kate that's what I thought, though, because (a) I was willing to bet that, in her heart, she knew it wasn't right. And (b) what can you do after the event? It's done, you can't rub out a tattoo, and you can't change having being late without saying you will be, after you have been.

I don't know why she wouldn't admit she was sorry for not saying anything, though, even though she must have been. It was almost like she was trying to punish Mum and Dad for something. But I can't think what.

4

I got to talk to Kate again after dinner. Well, after Mum had stormed off to bed and we'd pushed some food around our plates for a while and pretended to make conversation with Dad – if you can call *that* dinner. Then I went upstairs and sat on my bed and thought about homework, but I couldn't settle to anything. And I'd just decided to go up and talk to Kate when I heard her coming downstairs – not galumphing like usual, though, she was walking quietly. I bet she didn't want Mum to hear and pop out and grab her for another round of arguing.

Kate stuck her head round my door.

'Sorry about that, Mini darling,' she said. 'I know how you hate it when they argue. My fault.' Then she sat down beside me and hugged me. She's an excellent hugger; I felt soothed right away.

'Why didn't you tell them?' I asked. 'I don't mean about the tattoo,' I added quickly. 'I think you have every right to get one if you want. But about being late home?'

Kate sighed and rubbed tenderly at her shoulder.

'It still hurts a bit,' she said, wincing. 'Not that I'd admit that to *them*. So don't say, will you?'

'Of course not!'

Kate sighed again. She had a mixed expression on her face, like she was feeling two different things at the same time. I could see that she was upset, but she was pleased about something, too. She almost looked triumphant. I don't suppose that makes sense. It didn't make sense at the time, either. Because, to be honest, this wasn't the Kate I was used to.

Then she shrugged, like she'd made a decision. *A decision not to tell me something*, was what flashed through my mind.

'I couldn't *say* this morning, because I didn't *know* this morning,' she said. 'Not until after I left.'

'What, you didn't know you were going to get it done? Like, it was a spur of the moment thing?'

Kate hesitated, and then nodded. That seemed strange to me, but still, I thought it was possible. You go to school, you decide to get a tattoo, and then you go and do it. Just like that.

Then I had another thought.

'Did anyone go with you?' I asked. I suddenly

wondered if this was a Johnny thing. Kate looked at me sideways, gave a reluctant little grin, and then dropped her eyes.

I took that as a yes.

So maybe this was all about a boy? About Johnny?

I wanted to know more, but I felt slightly uncomfortable about asking. Kate hadn't actually mentioned Johnny by name so the someone who'd gone with her could have been one of her girlfriends. I could have got entirely the wrong end of the stick. I felt almost shy about it.

'I knew I was going to do it later on,' Kate offered. 'And then I thought about calling Mum, or even Dad at the office, to say I'd be late.' She gave another sigh and shifted around on the bed. 'But then – oh, I just couldn't be bothered by then,' she went on. 'I'd have had to tell a lie, because I knew they'd go ballistic about the tattoo, and I couldn't get up enough energy to go through all that, either.' She shrugged again.

I looked at her. What she'd just said didn't sound at all like Kate. It was like she was another person. But then she grinned mischievously at me, like the Kate I knew and loved so much, and patted my shoulder.

'Do you like it?' she asked.

'The butterfly?'

She nodded.

'I think it's great.' Well, I did. 'Why a butterfly, though?' She paused for a moment, and glanced at me like she was about to tell me something important.

But all she said was, 'Because it's a symbol of change.'

I didn't get it. If that was the important thing, well, I didn't understand.

'You mean, you *want* to change?'

For a moment Kate looked very sad, and when she answered it wasn't really to the point, it sounded like she was thinking about something else. And it didn't explain what she was talking about, either.

'Sometimes they just happen, Mini – changes, I mean. Whether you want them to, or not. You might not even know something's changed – it can sneak up and surprise you. Or things shift around when you're not looking, and it turns out they aren't how you thought they were. That's all.'

Clear like mud, right? I wanted her to explain better but then she leaned back against my pillows and smiled at me.

'Have we got to the oasis yet?' she asked.

I knew this was her way of changing the subject, telling me she didn't want to talk any more. I grinned right back at her.

'We just arrived,' I said. 'What do you think – should we eat around the camp fire?'

'I'm not that hungry,' said Kate. 'I can skip the meal tonight. Do you want me to take the first watch?'

The first watch would get her extra points, and I almost agreed she should do it just to keep her happy, when I remembered the raiders who were going to sweep down on their racing camels. I shook my head.

'Nope, I'll do it,' I said. I wanted to give her a surprise, and to be honest I was pleased that it would be one. I'd never thought up marauding raiders before. And she'd caused a fuss and a half that night, so I thought she deserved something unexpected. Which shows that I *do* understand about wanting to get back at someone, in a little way. Even at Kate.

I still don't get why she'd want to get back at Mum and Dad in such a way. They're really not that bad, as parents go.

But with all the tattoo fuss and everything, I didn't remember to tell Kate about Satch and the cupcakes. But I think the success of my Satch plan must have inspired the way I handled the raiders on their racing camels.

Kate was truly surprised by the whole episode,

and she shrieked with fright in a very satisfactory way when I pointed them out as they swept down from the mountains. And afterwards she said she really admired how I'd tricked them into thinking there were more of us than them. I let them creep into the oasis unchallenged and I left it until absolutely the last moment before I led our counterattack. It all worked out perfectly. She didn't even complain that I got so many extra points.

At the end of that week Mum had a cupcake emergency. The friend who helps her was on holiday, and Mum got way behind with the department store cakes. They had to be delivered on time the next morning no matter what, so I offered my services after school.

The job needs to be done just so, and Mum didn't used to let me or Kate help; she thought we wouldn't get things exactly right. We surprised her, though. We're really good at it now, and we often help even when she hasn't got behind with it all. We do moan on from time to time about child labour, and about how she's exploiting children down in the basement cupcake mine. But she knows we're teasing her, and she's relieved that we can lend a hand.

You might think: how difficult can icing little cakes actually be? Well, you'd be surprised.

For a start, the buttercream icing has to be exactly the right consistency – not too sloppy, or it slips down the sides and doesn't stay on top of the cake where it belongs.

And you have to get it exactly thick enough – no less than half a centimetre of icing. Less than that looks mean-spirited, Mum says. And more than that looks fine but uses up the icing too quickly, which cuts into Mum's profits. Mum's tried out different techniques to get the amount right every time, and now we use a small ice cream scoop to measure the icing out on to each cake.

Most of all, the job has to be neat. Not as neat as a machine would do it, because they're *supposed* to look as though they're made by hand. But they do have to be tidy. No dribbles down the sides, no blobs of icing oozing out. You get into the swing of it after a while. It used to take me ages to ice a whole tray of cakes, but now I can do all ten in no time if I really concentrate.

You might also think that if you get them wrong that's a *good* thing, because you can eat the mistakes. I thought that before I did it. But when you're on the spot you don't want to cheat and get them wrong so you can eat them; you just want to do the job right and take pride in your work, even if it's just icing cupcakes. Anyway, Mum always lets us have a couple of cakes when we help her – it's other times that she makes a fuss about it. I think she sees the ones we have when we're working as our wages.

While I was helping her Mum didn't say much, partly because she knew I was concentrating, and partly because she was, too, working on a new cake flavour to try out. She already does two: chocolate cake with chocolate or peppermint icing, and lemon cake with lemon or coconut icing. Now she wants to add another one. I voted for ginger, which is a flavour I like a lot, but Mum decided to try vanilla cake with orange or lime icing.

When she finally had a new test batch in the oven, and had mixed up both of the test icings and put them in the fridge, she took off her apron, washed her hands, and sat down with me at the bench. I thought she'd want to talk about Kate's tattoo. But what she actually asked me about was school.

So I told her about Satch and his stammer, and how I had got him to talk, because she likes to keep up with what we're doing at school and this was something new. Also, sometimes she worries about me not having friends, so I thought she'd be pleased to hear about Satch as a potential friend. Which he may be, although it's early days.

Mum's a lot more like Kate than she is like me,

although I don't think either of them knows that. They don't look much alike but they're interested in the same sort of things, where I am not. For instance, Kate has about a million very close friends and so does Mum. That's not necessarily better than how I am, or anyway I don't think so. I think it's just different. And they're interested in the same things as their friends and they spend a lot of time talking about them.

If I had a million friends they'd all have to be keen on geography, and what's the chance of that?

Mum says my interests will change once I am a fully-fledged teenager, and for all I know she's right. Maybe one morning, in just under five weeks' time, I'll wake up as a teenager and find that I care more about nail polish and dyeing my hair than, for instance, exactly where the San Andreas Fault Line runs. (From the west coast of the United States, then under the Pacific Ocean right across to Japan and down to New Zealand, which is why those places all have high earthquake potential, in case you're interested.)

But right now I don't see the point of most of what Mum and Kate talk about. When they're getting along OK they go on and on until I could frankly pass out from boredom. So in a way I wish I did care, and then I could join in. Or be less bored.

So I was pleased to have something to tell Mum that would interest her. She laughed when I told her how Satch makes up lists in his head, and she said it brought back an old memory for her about *her* mother – that's my grandmother. It turns out that she, my grandmother, had done something similar to conquer her shyness when she'd been Kate's age and going to dances.

'She used to knit a sweater in her head!' Mum said, giggling at the thought. 'She'd be off, purling and plaining her way along the rows of wool, and too busy to be shy. And she'd whirl around the dance floor in the arms of some young man, and he'd think she was fascinating and mysterious because she didn't say much, but she was just thinking about the sweater! Or so she said.'

I was still expecting Mum to ask me about Kate but she didn't, she had to rush off to deliver some cakes for a party. So I stayed downstairs until the vanilla samples were done, and then I put them on a rack to cool, ready to be iced. I was just about to go upstairs when Dad came down looking for me. His face brightened when he saw the cakes.

'They're not for us,' I warned. 'They're the new flavour Mum's trying out.'

'But we're her focus group, right?' said Dad, picking up the nearest one. 'So she'll want to know what we think, won't she?' He broke a piece off and popped it in his mouth, and then he closed his eyes like a wine tester on TV.

'Hmm,' he murmured, waving the rest of the cupcake under his nose like it was a glass of wine.' A hint of citrus, and just a slight aroma of—'

'Vanilla.' I finished the sentence for him, took the rest of the cake out of his hand before he could stop me, and ate it myself. 'It's vanilla, Dad.'

And not bad at all, I decided.

I could tell that Dad wanted to talk to me, and I was willing to bet it would be about Kate. And this time I was 100% right.

'Have you talked to our Maxi in the last couple of days?' Dad asked, sitting down at the bench and patting the stool next to his.

I sat down, looked at him, and put on my best *you must be joking* face. How could he imagine that I wouldn't have talked to Kate? Every day, every minute we were in the same place, just about – we talk all the time. When Kate was on a field trip last term and we couldn't talk, we texted each other instead.

'Yeah, well, wrong question really,' Dad admitted. 'I know you two talk all the time. But the reason I ask…' and he paused for a minute and fiddled around with a stack of mixing bowls on the bench.

He looked slightly embarrassed, which isn't like him. Dad usually says what he thinks to people straight out, and no messing around.

'Well, she's been awkward recently.' He turned his coffee cup round so the handle was lined up with the spoon, and then turned it back again.

'You mean the tattoo?' I suggested. But Dad said it wasn't just that.

'I don't know...' he said vaguely. 'But – well, she's unusually quiet, for one thing.'

I thought about that. Kate's the kind of person who waits and thinks things through before she complains. But now I wondered: had she been quieter than usual lately? Before the tattoo, I mean. I didn't think she had.

'Has she said anything to you?' Dad went on. 'About anything that's worrying her, or maybe something on her mind?'

He stopped fiddling with the cup and teaspoon, and started playing with a set of measuring spoons instead. I wondered if he was trying to be a spoon-bender; Dad found a website last month about magic tricks, and he's been trying them out.

'Nothing like that,' I said. ''Nothing I know about, anyway.'

Which wasn't strictly true, because Kate *had* talked to me the night of the tattoo. The trouble was she hadn't made much sense, but I wasn't going to admit that to Dad.

But then I suddenly thought: last year I'd have known for certain what was wrong with Kate. Now, I couldn't be sure. Not completely, utterly sure.

So something between us has changed.

One example is how I feel she doesn't *really* want to play the travel game any more, like she used to. That wasn't what Dad meant but still, it was true. And my face probably showed I was having doubts, because Dad went on.

'You know, Sweet Pea, some secrets are OK. Everyone has little things they don't want anyone else to know. Me too, as it happens, like – oh, like when I was your age I broke my mother's favourite vase and I *never* admitted it. She always blamed the cat. Sad, but true.'

He grinned at the memory, but then he got serious again.

'But if you've got a secret about something important – and you'd know if it mattered or if it was serious, you'd know what I mean – well then, you'd tell me, right?'

And I nodded and said yes, I would tell him. I don't know if that's completely true, but then I don't know exactly what Dad meant, and anyway I don't suppose it applies to us.

I suppose what he means is, if one of us knew about a crime – or if we were planning a robbery or a murder, or something like that. Which we are not. As far as I know, our only secret is the travel game.

And then Dad asked me something truly weird.

We were coming up the stairs and he suddenly said, 'Kate hasn't started wearing any new jewellery recently, has she, Mini? Something round her neck?' He said it very casually, like it was just an afterthought, but it's a very strange thing to ask, isn't it? First of all it's a fuss about Kate's tiny tattoo and now it's a fuss about what Kate might be wearing around her neck!

I haven't noticed anything new around her neck and I have no idea why it would matter if there was something, but why not ask *her*, for pity's sake?

That night in bed I worked on the next bit of the game. After we'd finished off the raiders last week we talked about what would come next, and Kate suggested going to the Stone Tower, which we haven't done for ages.

The Stone Tower is a Silk Road legend, from hundreds of years ago. The story goes that the Stone Tower was where silk merchants from the east first met traders from the west, but no one knows exactly where it was. No one even knows for sure if it's a true story – if the Stone Tower really existed. But I think it's probably true, and one day Kate and I are going to travel the Silk Road for real, and find the Tower – what's left of it, anyway. And I bet we can. The extra iron that Dad says I have in my nose will probably help with directions. And Kate's not good at geography but she's ace at almost everything else, so we're bound to succeed.

And when we go we'll ride camels for real, and not just in our imaginations. Like Kate always says, there's no better way to travel over sand.

But the thing is, the Silk Road wasn't an actual road at all and it wasn't even just one route. You didn't *have* to go through Tashkent or Samarkand, for instance – we only go that way because I like the names. I expect they're not glamorous or romantic places these days; they've probably got ring roads and motorways and supermarkets now. But in my imagination they're still as lovely as they were when the silk traders first travelled there, and I wanted to explore the countryside a bit and look for the Tower. So I decided we'd head north from the oasis along a river, through cherry and almond orchards, all the way to where I thought the Tower might be.

I fell asleep thinking about it.

5

The next school night I helped Mum clear the table after dinner. It's a job I'm supposed to do some nights and Kate other nights – it's all on the wall planner – and we usually end up doing it together, but Kate really did have dance after school so she was expected to be late.

This time her class was on the wall planner. 'Known in advance and cleared for take-off' is what she'd said that morning on her way out of the door. I thought she was pushing her luck because her tone of voice would normally get Mum into a spin right away, but she got away with it. No one's even said she's grounded, which usually happens if we're late without saying. It happened to me one time when all I did was stay and watch a football match without having said I would.

Wouldn't you think that three and a half hours

late *plus* a tattoo would be worse than that? And wouldn't you also think that my interest in sport was a good thing, and that any halfway reasonable parents would encourage it instead of making me stay home every night for a week?

But like I say, nothing's happened to Kate – not yet, anyhow. I don't *want* it to, though; I'd never wish a bad thing for her.

Anyway, it turned out that Mum finally wanted to talk to me about Kate. I didn't want to, though, and this is something I resent. It's like Mum and Dad sometimes try out ideas about Kate on me instead of starting with her. Almost like they're scared of her, except that's a ridiculous idea.

It's very unfair to go on at someone about things they *didn't* do and aren't responsible for. I hate Mum moaning on to me about Kate's faults, and Dad asking me about her jewellery. I want to say, *Go to the person who caused the trouble and ask them about it, and leave me in peace*. And of course I don't say that; it would just make things worse. But I think it.

So when Mum finally mentioned Kate's tattoo I said what I thought – that it's tiny and pretty, and in my opinion Kate should be able to do something like that without getting into trouble.

Mum looked surprised, like she'd expected me to agree with her about it, but why would I? She knows how it is with me and Kate.

'You don't *really* think that, do you?'

I nodded firmly.

'Yes, I do.'

'But Mini darling, can't you see? A tattoo sends completely the wrong message to the world.'

I started to feel uncomfortable as well as cross. I didn't want a lecture about tattoos; I wasn't the one who'd gone out and got one. And then I remembered Satch and his lists. It was worth a try.

Tashkent. Samarkand. Bukhara.

That was three, but what comes next? Is it Nishapur? Or maybe Ferghana?

I can't remember!

Maybe I should just start again.

Tashkent...

But Mum was well away by then.

'We're your parents, for heaven's sake' she was saying. 'And you're both interesting young women with minds of your own – for which I'm thankful, although you mightn't believe that right now. But...' and then Mum tapped my shoulder to make sure she had my attention; it was almost as if she knew I'd been trying to make lists in my head to distract myself. I should never have told her!

I gave up.

'But while you live at home,' she said firmly, 'you

have to follow the rules. We *all* agreed them, and so we *all* have to follow them.' She looked at me expectantly.

'But why all the fuss about a tiny tattoo?' I asked. 'There isn't a rule about those, is there?'

Mum opened her mouth to say something. Then she changed her mind and closed her mouth again into a thin, cross line, and got up to start the dishwasher. I knew she hadn't finished with me, though, and I wondered what it was she hadn't said.

There's something she's not telling me! I thought. *Just like Kate!*

It's not a good feeling when you think your family's ganging up on you. I know you might think I was being difficult too, but as it happens I was actually interested in what Mum's answer would be.

There couldn't be a family rule about tattoos. We'd never specifically agreed, as a family, that none of us would get tattoos without asking. And then I had another thought. How come Mum and Dad argue so much, then? There's certainly a rule about being considerate and courteous.

I didn't *say* any of that; I don't push things as far as Kate does. But I was feeling stressed out again so when Mum came back and sat down I wasn't looking forward to more of the same.

The Pacific Ring of Fire volcanoes might be easier.

I can always remember Cold Bay because it's such an unlikely name for a volcano, so I could start with that.

Cold Bay.
Mount Fuji in Japan.
Krakatoa's another one.

...

Oh, maybe I'm just rubbish at lists.
I gave up again.

'You two have to play fair with us,' Mum was saying. 'You can't go off doing your own thing without sparing a thought for others. Coming home four hours late without so much as a by your leave or an entry on the planner, let alone an apology.'

I sighed.

'Three and a half hours, Mum, not four,' I pointed out. 'But OK, I do see what you mean about that,' I added. I meant it, too.

'But why are you still on about a teeny weeny tattoo on Kate's shoulder?' I asked again. 'Isn't that a bit over the top? Lots of people have them these days, and not just rock stars and hip hop kings, either.'

Mum looked at me thoughtfully.

'Here's another way of explaining,' she said. 'If you start down that road it's hard to stop. And if you don't stop – if you go a long way down it – then you mightn't remember how to get back again.'

That sounded like geography to me, which was interesting. But I still didn't get it, and my face must have shown that because Mum sort of gave up.

'I'm sorry if you don't understand, Mini,' she said stiffly. 'You will one day, when you have children of your own.'

I ask you! What is she like? How does saying things like that help?

I took a calming breath.

'Look Mum, I agree that Kate should have told you she was going to be late. Definitely. But not about the tattoo.'

And I don't understand all this drama-queen fuss that you're making is what I thought, but didn't say.

'But Kate's been so strange just recently,' Mum said.

It sounded like what Dad had said to me.

'I think she might be acting out about something,' Mum went on. 'And I'm worried where it will lead.'

'Acting out? With one tiny tattoo?'

'Yes, Mini,' she said firmly. 'One tiny tattoo, as you say. It could be the first step down the wrong path.'

She changed the subject then, which was a relief, but I *still* don't get what she's on about. Kate is a teenager, after all, and I know what that involves, because (a) I live here too, and (b) I've heard Mum and Dad going on about them often enough. Teenagers try to push against the rules. That's what they do. I mean, I do it sometimes too, and I'm not even a teenager yet, although there's less than five weeks to go now.

A couple of years ago Mum made an enormous fuss when Kate announced that she'd gone vegetarian. Mum went on and on about it, like she was doing about the tattoo. And she'd said back then how she, that's Kate, had to follow the rules, although as far as I knew we never said we'd all eat meat. And anyway, being veggie is a conscience thing, and if that's what Kate's conscience tells her to do then she should go ahead. It would be wrong not to, in my opinion.

Anyway, after flying off the handle and making all that fuss and bother, Mum actually ended up by *agreeing* with that decision! And now she thinks that Kate's doing an excellent job of the whole veggie bit and making sure she gets enough protein and stuff. And she often cooks special veggie meals because of Kate, which actually means that a lot of the time I have to eat veggie meals too, and Dad, of course. I'm not a veggie myself, although I might well become one later in my life. Right now I'm more of a fishetarian, but I do eat chicken, too. And bacon. I miss bacon when we don't have it because of Kate.

I expect that Mum will calm down soon. She'll probably end up saying what a nice tattoo the butterfly is, and we should all get one.

That's a joke.

But if I had a tattoo it wouldn't be a butterfly, I'd get a geography-related one. Maybe a compass? That wouldn't be as pretty as Kate's butterfly, though.

When Kate got home, Mum didn't say much to her. She certainly didn't mention the tattoo, or being late without warning or not saying sorry. It was sort of like she'd worked it all off on me for now. Later on I told Kate what Mum had said, but she just shrugged and didn't want to talk about it.

I started to worry more about her that night. I could definitely see she wasn't her usual self. I could even tell she was *trying* to be nice to me and that made me sad, because why would she have to try? She never had before. What I mean is, as a general rule she's nice to me because she likes me, not because she has to be.

We didn't play the game that night, we just talked, but even that was hard work at first. I don't think I'd ever felt that before in my whole life. I could tell that she was thinking about something else, and making an effort not to show it.

But then I told her Mum's story about her own

mum knitting in her head to avoid being shy. I remembered it, because the way Kate was behaving made me appreciate what it must have been like dancing with someone who was knitting a sweater in their head. Kate liked the story, and she perked up after that, as if she'd come back from wherever she'd been. So I finally told her about Satch and she was interested in him, too. She laughed when I said how tall he was – he must be almost as tall as Dad but he's only about half as wide. Like an upside-down paintbrush, I think, because he has a shock of hair that stands up on end, like bristles do. Not that I would say that to him.

'That's like Lee's brother, Johnny!' Kate said. 'He's so tall his family call him a long drink of water!' She looked at me, and laughed again.

Then she said, teasing me, 'If you two get to be friends, you and this Satch, you're going to look *so* sweet going around together. One of you a tall, thin paint brush, and the other just a little titchy thing!' She started tickling me and we both fell about laughing because she used to call me a little titchy thing years ago, when I probably was one. I'm not now, not really, but I'm still a lot shorter than Kate. Or Satch, come to that.

I don't care about me and Satch looking funny together, if we get to be friends and go around together. But it's useful to be warned ahead of time. That way Ruby won't get in first.

Anyway, then I told Kate what I'd been planning for the game, about going along the river and through the orchards. She seemed really interested, but she did say one odd thing.

We were talking about how many camels we'd need, and should we leave the bales of silk under guard at the oasis or take them with us? And we needed to decide if we could carry over the points we'd got already. I said yes, because I had more points than Kate and I didn't want to lose them. She ended up by agreeing even though that meant she'd start at a disadvantage, which shows how kind she can be.

And then Kate said, 'Why not sand?'

I was puzzled, I thought I must have missed something.

Why not sand?

She had to explain. What she meant was, why didn't we travel up over the sand dunes, instead of along the river? And when I pointed out that sand dunes were hard going, and anyway that was where the raiders came from, she wasn't put off.

She said, 'But we'll have the camels, Mini! No better way to travel over sand, you know that!'

'But don't you think the camels might like a break

from sand?' I said. 'It's hard work for them, even though their foot pads spread out to help them walk.'

You might not know it, but the pads underneath camels' feet act a bit like snowshoes in soft sand and stop them sinking. Kate knows that as well as I do, so I didn't get it. She usually leaves details like that to me.

It turned out that she was remembering a time years ago when we'd had a holiday on a beach up north, and how we'd built sandcastles and played on the sand dunes. I do remember that, as it happens, but only vaguely, and Kate thinks she was about seven, so I would only have been three or four. No wonder I don't remember much about it.

What I *do* remember is riding on a grown-up's shoulders along the beach and looking down into the waves. It must have been Dad's shoulders; I remember clutching on to his hair because it was scary being so high off the ground.

'When the raiders galloped across the sand dunes on their camels the other night, it reminded me of that beach,' Kate said. 'It's just an idea, Mini, but it might be fun. I love beaches.'

'And sand,' she added after a pause.

Later on, I realised that Kate had mentioned Lee's brother Johnny again. I wonder if she's keen on him, like I think she could be? The way she sounded when she said his name was different, like she knew him better than she was saying, or she had a secret with him. Something like that, anyway.

Maybe Johnny got a tattoo as well?

If she does fancy him it might explain why she didn't say anything straight out to me, because she doesn't when it's boyfriend stuff. Not that she's had many of them, but when she does she closes down about them. It might be she's shy, or maybe she thinks it isn't something for me to know about. I expect she's different with her school friends.

But I don't think that can be the whole problem at the moment. Fancying a boy doesn't make her unhappy – she usually gets all giggly.

I'm certain there's *definitely* something wrong with Kate. Something's making her unhappy and she isn't saying. What I don't know is (a) what it is, and (b) why she won't tell me.

6

I still don't know what the matter with Kate is, but that doesn't seem important now. Because what happened last night is so awful I can't think about anything else.

Mum and Kate had a terrible row, a show-stoppingly bad one. The worst ever. And then Kate stormed out of the house, and she didn't come back *all night*. We had the police round and everything. So no one got much sleep, and I spent hours crying and the rest of the night worrying, or having horrible dreams. I'm still all shaky and confused. It's like I'm inside one of those snow globes, the ones you shake and turn over and then the snow whirls around. I feel like that, shaken and stirred and turned upside down.

In the end it turned out that Kate was OK. She'd spent the night at Lee's – but Mum and Dad didn't find out that she was safe until way after they'd called the police. Lee's mum didn't phone to say that Kate was there until about midnight, because she didn't know. She only found out when she went into Lee's room to give her a late night kiss, thinking she'd be fast asleep, and found Kate there too, in a sleeping bag on Lee's bedroom floor.

She hadn't heard Kate arrive, because she – that's Lee's mum I'm talking about – had her book group meeting and she was shut in their living room with six other women talking about a book, not wanting to attend to comings and goings in the house. So she didn't.

When she found Kate, and then phoned Mum to say Kate was there and safe and wanted to stay and was that really OK, it was *hours* after Kate had stormed out of home. And in the meantime Mum and Dad were both in a desperate state. Dad had driven around all the local streets trying to see if he could find Kate and make her come home. And Mum had phoned everyone she could think of and knew the numbers for – including Lee as it happens, but Lee's mobile was switched off and their landline was engaged because Lee's dad was on the phone to California for his work. You don't realise how easily things can conspire to stop you finding out something, until they do.

By the time Lee's mum phoned there were two policewomen in our living room, drinking tea and talking to Mum and Dad, and looking at photos of Kate, and making soothing noises to Mum who could hardly speak at all, she was sobbing so much. Then Lee's mum phoned, and a sort of wave of relief ran through the house. It rolled right up the stairs and over me, too, where I was sitting on the stairs outside Kate's bedroom door, although I was supposed to be in bed.

I thought I'd feel better then, but apart from the relief of knowing that Kate was OK, I actually felt worse. Shaky and sick, mostly, but something else was rising in my heart. Something I'd never felt about Kate before, in my entire life.

Mum and Dad were rather embarrassed that they'd called the cops for no reason – but as the policewomen said, they'd had reason enough to make the call, and everyone was pleased that it had turned out to be a false alarm. The policewomen hugged Mum as they were leaving, and said things like, 'Don't worry, Tiffany, she's safe and well and that's all that matters.'

I always forget Mum's name is Tiffany until someone says it. There's a bit of me that expects other people to call her Mum as well, although I know that's silly. But as it happens I don't agree with the policewoman. I don't think that's all that matters.

Because Mum was out of order with what she said to Kate, which I will get to in a minute. But Kate shouldn't have stormed out the door saying what *she* said, and then staying out without saying where she was. And it's the second time recently she's done something that I don't agree with, and I *hate* that.

I hate that she's done something I don't think is right.

I hate that I didn't know where she'd gone.

And I hate seeing Mum and Dad in such a state, and so worried about her, which made me worried about her too. I imagined her run over, or alone in the dark with horrible people around, or kidnapped and held to ransom.

Or even dead.

Of course I'm pleased that she's OK, and just with Lee. But after the first rush of being pleased, what I felt next was cross and fed up. And then I also felt cross with her about her *making* me feel cross. So I was doubly cross, which I also resent.

Because she's not supposed to do that! Best friends don't let each other down, or if they do it's by accident and they're sorry, and they *don't do it again*.

It had all started just as we were finishing dinner, so I suppose I should be grateful that we'd got through eating a proper meal this time. I don't like missing meals, or feeling so anxious I can't eat. But I wasn't pleased to have an argument start up again. Because (a) I'd had a good day at school so I was feeling perky, and (b) it was Friday night so another school week was over which was another reason to feel perky, having the weekend to look forward to. And (c) we'd all sat down together to dinner, which I like. In fact, when I think about it, what happened next could edge up quite close to the top of my list of grievances – that our happy family mood only lasted as long as it took us to eat dinner.

School's been good all this week, mainly because of Satch. I think we are probably, almost certainly for sure, going to be friends. The new reason for thinking that is because he turns out to be good at jokes, and since I very much enjoy jokes myself this is a promising development.

Also, he doesn't seem to care that I am sometimes known at school as the Map Queen. I wouldn't have told him myself because it isn't a good nickname, but he found out because Ruby tried out a new tease aimed at both of us. We were all in the lunch room and Ruby kind of minced past the table where I was sitting with Satch, like she was a model on a catwalk – that sort of mincing – and then she turned and pointed at us, and shouted, 'Hey, it's the Map

Queen and the North Pole!'

Satch didn't turn around, or twitch, or even blink. There was no sign that he'd actually heard her, and I thought that he mightn't have heard, because of all the noise. I have to admit I turned and glared at her, so she knew right away that she'd scored with me. But then I switched to ignoring her, like Satch was doing, which paid off because Ruby didn't like me not showing any more crossness than just one single glare. You could see she was simply *longing* for more of a reaction. I didn't even have to start a list in my head.

When we had finished our lunch and were going out, Satch suddenly asked, 'Why are you the Map Queen?'

I just said, 'Because of geography.'

I'd have left it at that but then he asked, 'So what's with you and geography, Mini?'

So I had to explain. About how it was the thing I was most interested in and so I was good at it, and everyone knew that and thought I was weird. And how I'd won a national prize last year, which embarrassingly had been announced in assembly and made them a lot worse. All that. Satch just nodded and didn't ask anything else, which was a relief. Sometimes in the past, new kids have been nice to me because they think that being with a Map

Queen will be a good thing. When the penny drops and they finally get it – that it's actually a sign of unpopularity and nothing about being queen of the class – they tend to lose interest. Frankly, I would rather they'd never pretended to like me in the first place.

Satch didn't say anything for a few minutes. And then suddenly he said, 'Ruby's way out of order, you know. It's not the North Pole, it's the *South* Pole!'

I just stared at him because I didn't get it, not right off. But while I stared Satch stopped walking like he usually does, which is a kind of a long-legged lope, and started walking *exactly* like a penguin. Short little steps, feet turned out and close together, arms tight to his sides like tiny wings. The full thing.

It was amazing. You could really *see* a penguin. And I burst out laughing, but Satch kept straight-faced like nothing was going on. And then he stopped being a South Pole penguin and went back to loping along like a too-tall twelve-year-old again, and never said another word more about it.

I heard him stammer when he said 'South Pole', but only a little bit. Just on the P of Pole. If I hadn't been listening hard I'd never have picked it up.

We spent the rest of lunchtime in the library. Satch mooched around and I played on a computer looking up sand dunes and river valleys for the Silk

Road. I also remembered the trouble I'd had listing Pacific Ring volcanoes so I printed it out, in case I met any more stressful situations in the near future.

Have you ever had a friend where you didn't have to do the same things together, you could do different things in the same place and not bother each other, but you were still glad the other person was there? It was a bit like that for us in the library. I feel quite hopeful.

Any day now I plan to ask Satch about his name. The only reason I am still hesitating is that I have realised the likely consequences. If I ask him, I have to be prepared for him to ask *me* about *my* name. And I'm not ready to tell him that. Map Queen's enough for now.

Anyway, that night Mum's dinner was one of my veggie favourites, mushroom lasagne, which seemed a good omen at the time, although obviously it was not.

Dad was in a good mood too, partly because he likes mushroom lasagne, as well. And also because he *loves* it when we're all together as a family. It makes him so happy because he didn't have good times when he was growing up. Dad was adopted and he was miserable about that for years. He doesn't talk about it much, so I don't know the details. But I do know that's why he likes it when our family gets along well.

Even Kate seemed more relaxed than she had been earlier in the week, although judging from what happened later on I was probably wrong about that.

Mum was a bit tired, but she was OK at first. We were all laughing and joking and swapping stories about our days. I'd never have guessed that we were perched on the edge of a precipice and about to fall right into it.

Or on the edge of a dormant volcano that is unexpectedly about to blow.

Or sitting happily together on a beach in the sunshine, although actually about to be swept out to sea by a raging tsunami.

The thing that caused the row was unbelievably small. It's hard to believe, now, that such a tiny thing could have done it.

Kate got up to start clearing the plates away.

You'd think that would have been a *good* thing in Mum's eyes, wouldn't you? But Dad hadn't quite finished eating when Kate got up, and Mum likes things to be done just so, which includes waiting at the table until everyone has either finished or excused themselves. So she raised her eyebrows as well as putting up a hand to signal to Kate that she should wait.

No biggie, really. But then Kate rolled her eyes to

signal impatience, and Mum took it the wrong way.

Well, I suppose the truth is that she took it the *right* way – the way that Kate intended – but also the *wrong* way, because she took it seriously instead of overlooking it.

So Mum got tight-lipped, and tapped on the table with her fingers in a way that even I thought was irritating, like she was laying down the law. And then Kate tapped the table right back at Mum, sort of mocking her, with her eyes narrowed and her hair tossed back in frustration.

The situation might still have been saved if they'd both just kept up their little mime show, instead of talking. I don't think you can insult someone to their hearts or hurt their feelings forever, with a mime.

Dad was still munching away at his apple. He hadn't picked up that there was trouble brewing; he didn't even notice what was going on until Mum took it a stage further.

She leaned forward over the table and said, all tight-lipped, 'Leave it, Kate! You know the rules!'

And Kate hissed, 'Typical! You really are the world's leading control freak, *cupcake lady*!'

I still think that "cupcake lady" *could* have been funny. It sounded it at the time, and in that split second of waiting for Mum to reply I could imagine her smiling about it. But boy! I am glad I didn't laugh. Because Mum took it straight to heart.

'Cupcake lady? *Cupcake* lady?' she hissed back at Kate, standing up and leaning over the table so that her face was about a millimetre away from Kate's. 'How dare you insult me? Those cupcakes pay for all your little pleasures, young lady!'

And I agree that Kate was rude, she flew off the handle right away. She didn't even work up to it, which (a) isn't like her at all, and (b) was a big mistake. I can see all of that.

So off they went.

They were well away in a heartbeat, both shouting and carrying on and insulting each other, and no amount of Dad acting the peacemaker and telling them both to cool it for heaven's sake, and grabbing Kate and holding her back when she whipped around the table looking like she was going to hit Mum, made any difference at all. He could have saved his energy to finish his apple.

And what Mum finally said to Kate was not all that different to what she often says in arguments with us.

She said, 'And while you're under our roof, *madam*, you'll follow our rules! Every single one of them! Or you're out on your ear, and that's the truth!'

Even at the time I thought that *madam* said in

that sarcastic tone, might be as offensive as *cupcake lady*, and it turned out to be Kate's last straw. Well, probably not that exact word, but the whole bit about either following the rules or being out on her ear. Mum really didn't mean that. I know she didn't, and I'd be willing to bet that Kate knew she didn't, too. But for some reason it was like a red rag to a bull.

Kate sort of drew herself up and stood looking at Mum for a moment – with her hands on her hips, and head thrown back, and her eyes flashing daggers.

She's as tall as Mum now, I found myself thinking. And what I noticed, in the way you can do while something else is going on and you only think about it again afterwards, was how sure of herself she seemed.

She wasn't going to give in, I could tell.

'Oh, it's time for the truth now, is it?' Kate said, with a cold little nod. 'Well that's fine, because I've had it up to *here* with lies anyway,' she added, waving her hand around at about the level of her tattoo. 'So I might as well go now, it'll save you the trouble of throwing me out!' And then she whirled around and ran upstairs.

Mum said, 'Oh, for pity's sake!' and stamped her foot in frustration. Dad patted her on the shoulder, and said soothing things. But I was frightened because I knew that Kate was really going and I didn't know how to stop her.

I could see that Mum and Dad didn't realise she actually meant it. They just thought she'd flounced off to her room, and they'd wait until she calmed down and then maybe have another talk and soothe the situation. So they were dismayed when she came back down about ten minutes later, with her coat on and her backpack over her shoulder. You could see that she'd been crying, but she wasn't any more. She looked furious, and I know that she was, too, which accounts for why she then said what she did.

It's the sort of thing you say in the heat of the moment, and it isn't necessarily anything you truly mean, not in your heart of hearts.

But shouting at Mum and Dad that they were hopeless parents and a complete waste of space, and why hadn't they just given her back – well, it was cruel. And she sort of *spat* it at them, which seemed to make it even worse.

They're not perfect, I freely admit that. I have many complaints about them, as I have said before. But I know they try, and I know that they love us.

And anyway, how could they possibly give us back? Give us back to where? To heaven, or something? That's just plain silly.

But Mum and Dad didn't think it was silly. They kind of froze in their tracks and stared at her, horror-struck. Dad even sort of reeled back for a moment like he'd been punched. And while they were both just standing there not saying anything in reply, and I was standing with my mouth hanging open but not saying anything either, Kate opened the front door, and – well, she just left.

She didn't even slam the door; she just pulled it softly closed behind her. Like closing a book you'd finished and hadn't much enjoyed. It sounded very final.

And what was worst for me was, she didn't look at me or say goodbye. It was like I didn't exist, or that I didn't matter to her.

And I know that's not true, I even knew it wasn't when she did it, but still, I felt crushed into tiny pieces.

7

So then came all the awful bits I've already mentioned, with Dad driving around looking for her and Mum on the phone, and the police, and then finally, Lee's mum's phone call.

The next day we were all exhausted. I expect Kate was too, although she wasn't around to look bleary-eyed and drop the loaf of bread on the floor because of having fumbling fingers, like the rest of us. She was still at Lee's place.

Kate arrived home just after lunch. Mum had been on the phone to Lee's mum for ages in the morning, and I think she talked to Kate as well. I knew from the bits I'd overheard that Kate was coming home, but I didn't know when. I might have guessed she'd arrive with a whole posse of friends to protect her, but all I'd been thinking about was what we'd say to each other when she finally turned up.

The front door slammed just after I'd loaded the

dishwasher, and a burst of conversation and clatter spilled through the house like a wall of sound. I leaned around the kitchen door to see who'd arrived.

Kate and Lee, plus a boy I didn't know, and two more girls, Tracy and Jess, who were a regular part of Kate's group. And an older boy I knew was Johnny because I recognised him after all. All of them were dumping their bags and coats and talking at once. I guessed they were making the noise to cover up any awkwardness for Kate, but I expect they all talk at once anyway.

Kate was sitting on the stairs taking off her boots, and then she looked up and saw me. She grinned at me and got back on her feet, and I'm sure she was going to come over and talk to me but Mum came up behind me, and Kate's face changed. Not to a cross face, more of a wary one. A sort of *What's going to happen now* face.

I have to admit that Mum handled it well. It could have been awkward, after Kate storming out and causing so much grief, but she was pretty cool about it. She welcomed Kate's friends, and then she gave Kate a quick kiss on the cheek, like Kate'd been out shopping for a couple of hours instead of out all night without saying. And then she held Kate's face for a moment in her hands, looking at her in a loving way, and just said, 'Later, OK, darling?' Kate nodded, and then they all went up to her room to listen to music. Well, not Mum of course, just Kate and her friends.

Before she went upstairs Kate came over and gave me a quick hug and whispered, 'I owe you, Mini.' But I still felt miserable and I didn't want to admit how cross I was with her, even to myself. So I felt confused, almost itchy. Like I couldn't settle to anything. I blamed the fact that I was tired, and I blamed the loud music coming down from Kate's room, but I knew those weren't the real reasons. The real reason was: why wasn't Kate explaining to me why she'd done what she did? Why wasn't she saying, for instance, *The reason I left the house without a word to you, not even looking at you, is...*

I thought of going up to Kate's room and joining them, but I didn't. I didn't want to look like a boring little sister tagging along for the ride; that would make me feel worse instead of better. Kate's friends mightn't even act that way – I'd often stuck around when they were there and they were nice to me, they always included me in their conversations and asked my opinion about stuff they were discussing, like I was one of the gang. But today felt different.

I didn't want to sulk, but I knew that I was. I hadn't ever resented Kate spending time with her friends before, but now it was like I was three years old and someone had taken away my favourite toy. I'm not exactly proud of that, but it's true.

And that thing Kate had said the night before, about being sick of lies? I didn't know what she meant. Maybe it was just something to say when she felt like being mean? But on the other hand, what was going on *right that minute* felt as bad as the worst sort of lie anyone could tell.

I tried reading a book about volcanoes to distract myself. The prize I won last year – the one that made Ruby call me Map Girl all the time instead of just some of the time – wasn't about maps at all. You could choose your own topic, and the one I chose was the history of an earthquake. I chose the San Francisco earthquake because it's very interesting – although maybe that isn't the word you'd have used if you'd actually been in San Francisco on 18th April 1906. You wouldn't have said, 'Wow! This is an interesting earthquake!' while you were running for your life to get away from the collapsing buildings, or from the fires that swept across the city afterwards. But now, looking back from the twenty-first century, that's what I think it is. It's an earthquake that taught people a lot about them, and how to be prepared for future ones.

Anyhow, I'm thinking about entering the

competition again. Volcanoes have become my new geographical passion, so I might write about them. Or hurricanes; I could end up choosing them, instead. Anyway, once I've chosen my subject area I need to work out how to put a winning project together. It takes a lot of time so I'm not absolutely sure I want to go through it all again. Winning was fun, though.

At first I couldn't concentrate on the volcano book but I got swept away as I read it. I don't know how much you know about volcanoes. For all I know you might be like Ruby and her friends, and sneer at anyone who cares about things like that. But I promise: they're amazing once you know about them: dangerous and wonderful. There are even underwater volcanoes in the deepest parts of the oceans, as tall as Mount Everest. Just imagine!

I'd almost forgotten I was unhappy until I heard voices and footsteps on the stairs: Kate and her friends were thumping back down past my room. I heard them putting on their coats in the hall and then shouting goodbye to Kate, who didn't need shouting to because she was right there with them, for heaven's sake. And then there was silence, followed by the kitchen door banging. I guessed that Kate had gone to talk to Mum.

That's when I decided I'd waited long enough. I

was completely and utterly sick of being the little sister, patiently sticking around to be on hand to be apologised to when Kate got around to doing that. So I decided to walk down to the public library and see what they had on volcanoes. The school library's OK, but the public library in the shopping centre has a bigger reference section, plus DVDs and videos to borrow.

I put my head around the kitchen door before I left, to tell Mum where I was going – and OK, also to check what was going on with her and Kate. They were sitting at the table with some papers spread out in front of them, which was a bit strange. I thought they'd be talking about the night before, not going through shopping lists.

They suddenly stopped talking when I came in, and Mum quickly shuffled the papers together, which was even stranger.

And then she said, 'We're going through subject options for next year,' at the *exact same time* as Kate said something about needing ideas for her dance class.

Oh, right. How pathetic is that? Like I would believe either of them! Frankly, if they were both going to lie to me, I was glad to be out of it.

So I said what I was doing, and Mum offered to ask Dad to drop into the library on his way back to give me a lift home if I wanted one. I didn't know he'd gone into work, but he sometimes does at the weekends, just for a while. Anyway, Mum's suggestion suited me, because it meant I could stay at the library if I wanted to, until he arrived, and not if I didn't. Hanging around waiting for someone to do something had just shot to the top of the list of Things I Don't Like.

I felt better when I was walking down to the library. Mum would say it was because I was out in the fresh air, something she is very keen on, instead of shut up in my stuffy room getting a headache, which in fact I didn't have.

The problem isn't being shut in a room having a headache, I imagined myself saying to Mum. *The problem is our family, and the way we don't say what's really wrong. We go round and round in circles and don't tell the truth and never get anywhere, and it wears you out.*

Just thinking about it all made me feel upset again, so I tried to concentrate on volcanoes. I did pretty well on that the rest of the way to the library, even without trying to make a list in my head.

And as soon as I walked in, I saw Satch! Somehow I don't have him down as a keen reader so I was surprised to see him, although he was actually leaning against the wall, listening to his iPod with his eyes closed, and not choosing books at all. I walked over to him, and he opened his eyes and grinned at me. He acted like we met in the public library every Saturday afternoon, and seeing me there wasn't a surprise. And when I asked why he was hanging around, he nodded at the children's book room.

'Little brother's just joined up,' he said. 'Sim's a bit of a reader; he's just learned how.'

Sim's eight, but he's smaller than I expected, or maybe he just looks small beside Satch. He came staggering across the foyer just then, almost hidden behind an enormous pile of books that covered just about all of him except for his feet.

'Look! I found all these I want to read!' he said. He sounded very excited about it. 'What do I do now, Satch?'

Satch turned him and the pile of books around and aimed him at the checkout desk, but Sim had a problem with one slippery book in his pile that kept slipping to the side. For a moment it looked like he was losing the battle and the whole pile was going to crash to the floor before he'd checked them out. But Satch reached out with one quick movement, grabbed Sim and straightened all the books out, and pointed Sim at the desk again. Then he turned back to me.

'Not enough books in the school library for you,

either?' he asked. 'That's Sim's trouble,' he added. 'He gets through more in a day than I read in a week.'

Satch was having a problem with B and G sounds in his words today. Maybe it was the stress of looking after Sim.

I started to explain about volcanoes and the competition. As soon as I began talking I realised that (a) I hadn't even told Kate, yet, about maybe entering the competition again, which was unusual for me, and she'd been such a help with the last one. And that (b) telling Satch about it was something I hadn't actually decided to do; I'd just launched into it without even wondering if he would think I was a sad geek, or if he would laugh at me.

If Satch had the sad geek thought, he didn't let it show; he just listened and looked interested. I have to say it's nice to be listened to. There's not enough of that going on in my family right now, as far as I am concerned.

I know more about Satch now including something unexpected, which is that he likes cooking! You'd never have guessed that; he's too thin to look like he's interested in food. TV chefs aren't exactly skinny, and Mum, for instance, she's not fat but she's not like a pencil either, she's sort of round, in a nice way.

Anyway, how I found out about Satch and food at the library had nothing to do with books; he didn't sneak off to the cookery section or anything like that. But when Sim finally checked out his books there was a new problem, which was how to get them all home. He and Satch had to divide up heavy things so Sim could manage his own backpack. And when they spread everything on the floor to reorganise it, Satch's backpack was full of food shopping! He had tins of tomatoes and bags of peppers and onions, and even chillies and garlic and ginger, which was a bit unusual. But then, so is Satch.

Sim saw me staring at the food and he said, 'Because he cooks! Satch cooks a lot! More than anyone else at our house! He's really good! Sometimes he lets me help!'

Everything Sim says sounds like it's surrounded with exclamation marks. He's very excitable. Satch calls him Longlife Sim because he's like a battery that goes on and on. I could tell that Sim wouldn't have stopped telling me and everyone else in the library how great his brother was, but Satch shut him up by asking him to try out his re-stuffed backpack. He could just about manage the weight, although his knees looked a bit wobbly to me.

Sim reminds me of how I must have been about

Kate when I was his age, rabbiting on all the time about how wonderful *she* was. He's rather sweet. I don't know that I was, though.

'So what's with the cooking, then? Are you going to be a celebrity chef?' I asked Satch, watching Sim parade around the foyer. As soon as the words came out I realised it sounded like I was teasing him – like the kind of thing people say to me about geography, though I didn't mean it like that at all. And I blushed; I could feel a big wave of red rising up from my neck all over my face. My cheeks felt they were on fire.

I muttered, 'Sorry, I didn't mean it like that,' but Satch had already started to tell Sim to tighten his backpack straps and the moment passed. I think he might have noticed me blush but I don't know if he'd heard what I said. I hope he didn't.

Anyway, we were still standing in the entrance when Dad walked in looking for me. Right away he said he'd drive everyone home, and I could see that Satch was pleased. Sim was over the moon because he had *another* new person to show off to.

'It's really heavy, this backpack! But I can carry it easy, look!' He must have said that to Dad a dozen times on the way to the car, and Dad was great every time. He's good with little kids, my dad. And he wasn't wearing his old red trousers, which was a blessing.

After we dropped Satch and Sim off, Dad asked me how I was.

'I'm OK,' I said. It sounded grumpier than I meant it to, but now we were going home I felt nervous again. I glanced at Dad, and decided to be brave.

'Are you and Mum going to sort things out with Kate?' I asked.

Dad reached over and patted my hand.

'Of course we are, Sweet Pea,' he said. He sounded calm and confident, which made me feel better.

But then he added, 'Tiff and Kate were talking everything through when you left, weren't they? Getting it sorted?'

I stared at him confused, before I remembered that he'd talked to Mum on the phone. But—

'They said they were talking about subject choices and dance class,' I pointed out. 'Not about getting anything sorted.'

I wondered what he'd say, but he just muttered, 'Oh, right,' and looked embarrassed.

So who's lying to me? Are they all doing it?

When we got back home Mum and Kate had finished talking – I could tell they'd only just left the kitchen because the kettle was still warm, and so were the empty mugs in the sink. I knew Kate must still be upset but I'd had enough of asking questions that didn't get straight answers, so I thought I'd let her find me when she wanted to talk.

Which she soon did.

She put her head around my door. I hadn't even heard her coming down the stairs, she'd been so quiet.

'Mini, I looked for you before,' she said in a wobbly voice.

She looked terrible, actually. White as a sheet, all sort of pasty, with big circles under her eyes that weren't mascara that had slipped. And while I was staring her face sort of crumpled up, and tears started to roll down her cheeks. She licked them off when they got down as far as her mouth, but they didn't stop coming.

'I'm sorry,' she sobbed, 'I didn't mean to make things hard for you, too.'

I hadn't seen Kate cry since she fell off her bike and broke her arm, when she was ten. She was too miserable to be bombarded with questions, and so I didn't ask her any although I was dying to. So we just sat side by side on my bed while I hugged her and she sobbed. She got the hiccups, she cried so much. But after a while she gradually stopped crying and we just sat hugging.

'What were you and Mum talking about?' I finally asked.

'I can't explain,' she said. 'I wish I could, Mini, but I can't.'

I just kept patting and stroking her, and of course worrying about her, and by then I was just about bursting for an answer, too, but I didn't say that.

And the other thing I didn't mention but I couldn't help noticing, was the silvery chain around her neck under her shirt. Kate's never worn a chain before – neither of us has one. Well, not before now, anyhow. But if that's what Dad meant when he asked me if Kate started to wear any new jewellery – well, I've decided that I'm not going to be the one to tell him. He can notice it for himself, like I did.

Then Mum called up the stairs that dinner was on the table. Kate went to the bathroom and washed her face, and then she came back and sniffed some more, and blew her nose. She'd more or less stopped having hiccups, which is the worst thing about crying a lot. That, and how bits of your face swell up and your eyes go pink.

Dinner wasn't as bad as thought it would be. Mum and Dad were too tired to talk much, and Kate was too upset, and I was too worried. So really, we just ate. It's amazing how much we all ate. Food can be a serious comfort in times of trial, it must be that.

Kate must have taken off her chain in the bathroom, because you couldn't see it when she bent down to pick a fork up off the floor. But I can't believe it matters, or that it's anything serious. Anyway, I bet Johnny gave it to her.

I'll get on with planning more of the Stone Tower journey now. I'll make it over sand, too, if Kate really wants that. If it will make her happy, then I'll go for it.

Because if Kate's happy, I'm happy. And if she's not, well, neither am I, even if I don't know what the problem is.

8

Kate still won't tell me what's wrong and I haven't nagged her about it. But I can't pretend I don't want to know because of course I do, and I have been developing some theories about it all.

A tiny bit of me thinks that it's disloyal to work it out behind her back. Maybe if Kate doesn't want to tell me I should accept that, and support her decision. But the rest of me can't bear to wait. It's not only that I'm naturally nosy and hate not knowing things, it's also because if I knew what was wrong I might be able to help solve the problem.

I have developed more than one theory, and I'm trying to work out which is most likely. I have thrown some ideas away already, like the idea that a friend of hers had turned into an ex-friend. Why would that be a secret? And it can't be that she's binned Johnny or he's binned her, because he was here the other day and stayed to listen to music. He wouldn't have done that if he and Kate were exes. And anyway, *that* wouldn't be something that Mum would spend hours talking to Kate about in the kitchen with papers spread out, and then have to have a lie down afterwards.

Having a bad time at school doesn't seem enough of a drama, either. Anyone can have a bad time at school; I do it myself sometimes. It doesn't make you cry so much that you get hiccups and your eyes swell up. So I started to think all over again, and put together some new ideas.

(a) She might have done something terrible at school and she's going to be expelled. That would tick most of the boxes that need ticking, but it seems unlikely. Kate has always been a bit of a goody-goody at school. She likes to please the teachers and make them think she's obedient even when she isn't, and as far as I can tell they're mostly sucked in by her, or even if they aren't they go along with her because they want an easy life too.

So, probably not that.

Or (b), Mum and Dad are going to take her out of school and put her in another one, and she doesn't want to go.

But why would they do that? It makes no sense. They're not likely to stick either of us in a new school for no reason. The only reason I could come up for that would be if we were expelled, which takes me back to (a) which I have already rejected as a likely cause.

(c) The silver chain that I saw around her neck is stolen, and the police are after her to recover the goods.

That one's so silly I can't believe it myself, even though I thought it up. If Dad thought Kate had received stolen property he wouldn't ask me to look out for it; he'd just make Kate give it back. And Kate wouldn't do that anyway – why would she? She could buy her own chain, like she bought her tattoo, although I still think Johnny probably gave it to her.

(d) Kate has witnessed a robbery or a murder, and she doesn't want to tell the police about it because then the robber or the murderer will know she saw what they did and will come after her, too.

OK, that isn't likely but it is *possible*, and I'm trying to cover everything. I have kept this idea in because of Dad asking me if we had a secret, so I thought of this as a reason to have an important secret. But in the cold light of day it sounds too much like a TV thriller and not like our real lives, which are generally rather ordinarily boring. Or anyway, they used to be.

(e) Kate has developed a deadly illness and she only has a few months to live, but she doesn't want to tell me because it will upset me.

That one's a bit far-fetched. She doesn't *look* sick, just unhappy. Also, surely everyone would realise that *not* telling me would be worse in the end?

But while I was just letting ideas arrive in my head and jump around in my imagination, I did come up with another possible cause that *could* be true. It seems more likely, and it ticks most of the boxes that need to be ticked.

What if (f) Kate's discovered that Mum and Dad are splitting up? What if maybe the papers on the kitchen table were divorce papers?

They do fight a lot, and when they fight they say things to each other that could be the cause of splitting up. Kate's friend Jess, well, her parents got divorced last year. And Jess told Kate, who told me, that her parents had spent months nagging each other about little things like leaving lights on, or running the water too long while they were brushing their teeth, or not taking their turn to put out the recycling.

You'd never think people could split up because of things like that, would you? But it looks like Jess's parents did. And that would *definitely* be something that Kate wouldn't want to tell me, if it was about Mum and Dad. She wouldn't want to upset me, especially if she thought they only *might* split up and she was still hoping they'd change their minds, before it was final and I absolutely had to be told.

I admit that this theory doesn't fit with what Dad said to me about having secrets. Because, why would Dad have asked me what was wrong with Kate, if he already knew? But I don't know the answer to that question. What I do know is, I would hate *hate* HATE it if Mum and Dad split up.
I wouldn't know who to choose to be with.

And what if Kate went with one of them and I had to go with the other?

That would be – no, I don't even want to think about it, it would be so awful.

I really hope that I'm wrong about this.

I worried about Mum and Dad splitting up for days until I couldn't bear it any more, so I went up to Kate's room and asked her straight out if it could be true. She looked very surprised. And she said no, of course not, and why on earth would I think that?

I still think that my idea about them *might* be true, and Kate just won't say. She is an ace liar when she wants to be, and although she says that this time she *isn't* lying – well, she would, wouldn't she? When I say Kate's an ace liar I don't want you to think she's a devious and awful person, because she isn't. The point is that when she does lie she's good at it, and people tend to believe what she's saying. It goes with her making teachers think she's a goody-goody, when she's actually not.

But she did point out that they don't argue any more than they ever did, and that's true. And then she said something else.

'Look, Mini, they've *always* shouted a lot when they disagree,' Kate said. 'I don't like it and you don't like it, and we've always wished that they wouldn't. Right?'

She waited for me to nod agreement, looking solemn.

'Right,' she said again, after I'd nodded. 'And it's never stopped them, more's the pity. But on the other hand, they fight less than they did when you were small. You probably don't remember?'

She sort of looked a question at me and I told her about remembering being outside with her in the garden, years ago. She nodded.

'See?' she said. 'It's not like that any more. I'm telling you, it used to be worse.'

She looked at me thoughtfully, and then she said, 'I'll tell you something to convince you, shall I?'

That sounded more like Kate. I nodded.

'I found out they were going to a counsellor for a while,' she offered. 'So they could learn how to stop arguing and get on better.'

'Why didn't you tell me?' I asked. Kate sort of shrugged a reply.

'I only knew because they put it down in code on the wall planner,' she said with a little smile. 'But I sussed it out.'

The little smile turned into a grin.

'I didn't tell you, though,' she admitted. 'I didn't want to worry you. And it wasn't a worry, as it happens. Lots of people sort out their problems by talking about them.'

'So why can't *you* do that, Kate?'

Kate looked at me. She had an expression I remember from years ago, when we played just about all the time. She used to put me to bed and read me stories, and she'd tell me off when I was naughty. It must have been like having a real live doll to play with – one you loved, and who loved you back.

Anyway, the look she gave me – it's hard to describe; it's a sort of full-on 100% attention look. And suddenly, I knew she was definitely going to tell me *right then* what was wrong, and why she was so unhappy.

I held my breath in anticipation but I suddenly wondered, *Do I really want to know?* That sounds weird, because of course I did. In my heart, deep down, I wanted to know. But a voice in my head said: *What if it's awful?*

Anyway, as it happened, she didn't. She went back to looking like Kate-these-days, who has a different expression on her face. More cautious and uncertain.

'Because I just can't,' she said softly. 'I can't explain. It's too much of a mess.'

I hated how that made me feel, and then she tried to explain another way.

'Do you remember those Russian dolls Mum used to have?' she asked. 'A painted wooden doll that you screwed open, and there was another one inside? And another one, and so on, smaller and smaller? Well, that's what this feels like, and that's all I can tell you right now.'

She patted my shoulder, and when she went on her voice sounded more confident.

'Anyway, don't worry, because I've worked out what to do. And whatever happens, Sweet Pea, it has nothing to do with you.'

My stomach lurched with fear.

'What do you mean, "whatever happens"?' I asked suspiciously. 'What's going to happen?'

Kate sighed, and patted my shoulder.

'It's just a turn of phrase, Mini,' she said. 'It doesn't mean anything – well, it doesn't mean anything *is* going to happen, anyway. All I'm saying is, don't worry.'

But I can't not worry.

When I remember all the complaints I have made in the past, about the things that are wrong in my life...

Well, they're nothing to what's wrong now.

I think I can even put up with my terrible name, at least until I am eighteen and can change it, if only Kate would be happy again.

Of course, I have thought of asking Mum or Dad to tell me what's wrong. And the reason I don't want to ask them is rather sad and pathetic, but it's true.

I don't want them to know that Kate won't tell me.

Kate *always* tells me things. And they know that. And I feel awful about her not telling me, almost as awful as I do just worrying about her.

What it *really* is: I feel embarrassed about one of those things and miserable about the other one, and I am not offering the world any prizes for guessing which is which.

So I can't ask Mum or Dad.

The next day I surprised myself by blurting out my worries to Satch. I didn't plan to talk to him about it. I didn't even know that I was going to until I'd started.

One reason why it's weird is that, I don't think I've *ever* told another person, except for Kate of course, anything that's a secret.

I can't actually remember if I ever told Joe anything secret or private, but I don't think I did. I probably didn't have many secrets worth sharing in Year One.

Satch, as I have said before, is excellent at listening. It's partly because he doesn't say very much, and that leaves space for other people to jump in. So when I heard myself starting to tell him how worried I was about Kate, I didn't stop; I didn't even hesitate. Which goes to show that when everything else seems to be changing, well, then so can I.

Satch didn't say anything until I'd finished explaining about how Kate was in trouble with Mum and Dad, and how she'd got a tattoo without saying she'd be three and a half hours late home, and how she'd run off and spent the night on Lee's bedroom floor, and Mum and Dad had called the cops before they knew where she was. And how ever since then she cried a lot and Mum was sad as well, and I didn't know what to do about it because no one was explaining, or even saying the same things about it when I asked them.

As I got to the end of the story my voice went a bit wobbly, but I am proud to say that I didn't cry, I just got a bit damp. I think Satch thought I might cry, though, because he bent down and fiddled with the strap on his backpack, which meant I could wipe my face without him looking.

We were in the public library again – Satch to return some of Sim's books, and me for the homework help club. I wouldn't have chosen the library as a place to talk but there we were, and I couldn't think of anywhere else to go to be private, and if you go into the Mixed Media Room you're allowed to talk if you keep your voices down. And usually there's no one else in that room anyway, don't ask me why, which makes it a useful place for confidences of a personal nature. If I turn out to make a habit of this I may well use it again.

Talking to Satch reminded me that being a good listener doesn't just mean you shut up and let the other person moan on. It also means that you seem interested in what they're saying, and when they're done, you try to say something helpful. Which is where Satch scored, because right away he had something to offer.

'Things are often difficult at my house, too,' he said with a sympathetic grin. 'Lots of shouting, and everyone coming and going all the time, like a railway station at rush hour.' He wasn't stumbling over any letters; it must have been a good day for his stammer. Or, a bad day for his stammer and a good day for Satch.

'I'll tell you what, though,' he went on. 'I don't like family dramas *any* time. People carrying on and flouncing off and then rushing back in for more shouting? All that? I just want to turn up the sound on my iPod.'

I felt better as soon as he said that. It made me wish that I had an iPod to listen to in times of stress, and right then I decided to alter my birthday list and put one at the top, ahead of the volcano book.

'Our house is, like, the family drama capital of the world,' Satch went on. 'Everyone's got something to sound off about. But we have this family conference every week. We all sit around the table and say what's on our minds. You have to take turns though. You can only talk when you're holding the spoon. Two minutes a go, max.'

He sort of gestured to show what holding the spoon was like: a two handed job, by the look of it. It must be a big spoon. I wonder if Mum and Dad had to take turns with a spoon when they went to see a counsellor.

'You don't always want to know what everyone's on about,' Satch went on. 'But it helps keep things straight. And it's only once every seven days; I can put up with that.'

I wondered if we could do that at home. There'd

been a time it might have worked, but I didn't know if we could all sit for long enough together these days without shouting or crying or running off. Or even if we'd all sit down together any more. It reminded me how bad things had got.

But Satch thought Kate was probably just having teenage troubles. 'Lots of them go through that stuff. My brother Tom, when he was Kate's age, couldn't stand being at home any more. He went and lived with Uncle Ted for a whole school year.' Satch shrugged. 'But he's back now – well, he's gone off again, but that's because he's at college and not because he's still sick of us. He just needed some space to sort his head out. He likes peace and quiet, same as me, which you never get at our place.'

I felt better when I was walking back home, because maybe my family wasn't that unusual? Everyone had problems, didn't they? You just had to ride them out.

When I got back home everyone was there. The house smelled of baking because Mum had been finishing a special cake order. Even though the cakes are not for me, coming in to the smell of them is always comforting.

And it was almost like Dad knew how bad I was feeling and he'd made a special effort to cheer me up. What he'd done was, he'd hired some DVDs for us to watch together. He'd actually got three, so there'd be at least one that we could all agree on. And he asked me to help make popcorn, which he'd got to go with the movies.

Kate was in her room, but she came down when I called up to her and we popped the popcorn together. We'd never made the fresh stuff ourselves before from the corn kernels; we've only ever bought it ready popped. It's a whole lot harder than you'd think because we didn't put the lid of the saucepan on tightly enough and when the corn swelled up it suddenly burst out of the saucepan and jumped all over the kitchen. We tried to catch the exploding popcorn and then we tried to pick it up, but once it's popped all over the bench and the floor and underneath the cupboards and in behind the washing machine you've had it; you have to start again. Luckily, Dad had bought two packets so we had a second chance, and this time we took turns to hold the saucepan lid down.

Kate was pretty quiet at first but at least she wasn't cross and her eyes weren't pink so she couldn't have been crying recently. And when the popcorn behaved like a wild thing she laughed as much as I did. We both ended up hiccupping with giggles, which is a whole lot better than hiccupping from crying too much.

Then Mum came up from the basement with a big chocolate cake she'd made and iced specially for us, as a surprise. She arrived with it like it was a big treat, which it was, and she stood in the doorway and said, 'Ta da!' and flourished the cake in triumph. The cake said *Happy Film Night* on it, in sprinkles. So we had cake *and* popcorn that night, and no one said a single word about healthy eating or vitamins, or that we should only have a little bit and save room for dinner. We all pigged out on popcorn and cake, and watched one and a half movies. One whole one, because although we'd all seen the first *Shrek* movie we found we could sit through it again very happily. You miss some of the jokes the first time round. Then we tried the same thing with the first *Toy Story* movie, which Dad had chosen for the same reason, although that didn't work as well so we only did half of it.

But the amazing thing was, we all agreed about both those things. And we were fine together, honestly, really quite OK. So when I went to bed I felt completely different from how I had only a few hours before, when I was moaning on to Satch.

I almost phoned him to say he was probably right about things sorting themselves out, and that I was sorry I'd been boring, but I don't have his number. I *still* don't know why he's called Satch, but I'm nowhere near ready to tell him my name so that's only fair.

9

That night, in bed, I wondered when I could start the Stone Tower journey, and whether Kate would actually do it with me. The thing is, I don't want to start without her if she definitely wants to do it, but I don't want to hang around waiting forever, either.

The whole film and popcorn thing the other night was fine. But I can see that she doesn't want to spend time with me at the moment like she did before. She isn't being mean. I can't imagine that she ever would be. She just isn't being Kate, not the person I've known for almost thirteen years, anyway.

For all of my life, actually.

Like when we both came upstairs after having a good time as a family tonight – well, as soon as we left the living room she went straight back to how she'd been earlier in the day. Sort of, like, *not there*. Like she'd used up all her reserves of family togetherness on the popcorn and the movies, and she didn't have anything left for her and me together.

I think it's the fault of whatever it is that she can't tell me. It sits in her mind like a hurricane on a radar map, getting bigger and stronger every minute, and she can't ignore it, it's too huge, and so most of the time she can't think about anything else.

So I decided to start the journey from the oasis while I was waiting to see if Kate would come too. I thought I might be lonely without her, but it was rather peaceful. I had lots of time to enjoy the scenery and listen to the sounds of the desert. You might think the desert would be completely silent, but in my imagination it doesn't turn out that way. There's the creak of the saddles, and the *thwump! thwump!* of the saddlebags against the camels' sides as they sway along, and there's the squeak of the sand dunes shifting under their hooves. I decided to turn up a river valley in case I didn't have a chance to do that when we were looking for the Stone Tower. I wanted the camels to have some shade, and enough drinking water to fill their humps.

It worked out fine, and I was glad I hadn't nagged Kate about doing it with me. The last thing I wanted was to start an argument with her; I didn't think I could bear it.

But I did keeping worrying about her. I was very

worried.

And as it turned out, I was right all along.

Because ten days later, Kate disappeared.

It wasn't like when she'd stormed out after the fight with Mum. This time there hadn't been a fight and there wasn't any special clue ahead of time. Nothing new, anyway.

She just didn't come home from school on the Friday. Dad was home that afternoon instead of Mum, and when he started ringing round to find out why she was late he found that she hadn't been in school at all that day. Actually, Kate's school had phoned mid-morning and left a message to say she hadn't been there for registration, and was she sick? But no one had seen the message light flashing because the answering machine's in the den, and Mum and Dad had been rushing around doing their yo-yo act and just never thought to look. Neither did I, because I was at school all day and Kate left just before me, like usual.

Everything had seemed fairly normal after the popcorn night – normal for how things had been recently, anyway. So I hadn't the faintest idea that she'd gone.

Still, I discovered that I wasn't all *that* surprised. You know how people say they're waiting for the other shoe to drop, when one thing's happened and they expect another one to follow? It was like that. The first shoe had been how Kate was behaving – to me, most of all – and so when this finally happened I knew it had been coming even if I hadn't predicted it.

I don't mean that I *wanted* Kate to run away. Of course I didn't. I only mean that, in a weird way, it was almost a relief, now it had happened. And maybe it's not like a shoe dropping; maybe it's more like what happens after a storm. I read about this the other day, in a book that had stuff about hurricanes and tsunamis as well as volcanoes.

Before a storm arrives the air pressure drops right down, and you can feel the difference in the air all around you. It makes you feel tired, or you think that you're getting the flu, and your head aches and you can't think straight. But after the storm when the air's cleared and the pressure rises again you feel better. Your headache goes, and you can think again.

And now something *had* actually happened, my head had cleared too. Kate disappearing was just about the worst thing I could imagine – but still, I didn't have to hold my breath any more waiting for it.

And what I thought was, *Now I can do something about it.*

I knew what I was going to do, too, after all the kerfuffle and hoo-haa had died down a bit.

I am willing to bet that Kate can't solve her problem without me. So I am going to track her down. I'll find her, and help her solve whatever it is, and then bring her home.

I didn't know how to find her but I knew I would, because I knew that I *had* to. I felt better as soon as I had decided, but still, I knew it would be hard to put my idea into action.

The first thing I had to do was *make* Mum and Dad tell me the truth about what had been going on. They went into a complete topspin about Kate disappearing, of course, and they're still in it. I'm as worried as they are, but at least I've got a plan and I don't think they do, not one they're going to put into action themselves, anyway.

They called the police again when they realised Kate had actually been missing all day. The same policewomen came back and talked to Mum and Dad for ages that night, and then again the next morning. They looked all through her room with Mum, and they talked to me, and then they talked to Kate's friends and the teachers at her school.

Her friends don't know anything, not even Lee or Johnny. Well, if they do they're not saying, but I don't think anyone *does* know, actually. They wouldn't keep it back now; it's too serious. This is a good example of the sort of secret you can't keep to yourself, if you have it.

But for me the most important thing – what I care about more than anything, and it might sound selfish but I don't care – is to have Kate back home for my birthday.

I couldn't *bear* it if she wasn't there. I'd rather not have a birthday than have one without her.

Nothing else matters right now in my life. I'd do anything. I'd put up an enormous billboard in front of the school with my real name on it in letters as big as a bus, if only that would happen.

When I said that no one knows anything about what's happened to Kate, I wasn't telling the entire and absolute truth.

I think that I might know something. Or rather, I think I have a clue.

I'm not sure it's a genuine clue. And even if it is one I don't understand it. But it's somewhere to start.

The night after Kate went – last Friday night – I found something in my room. When I finally got to bed, after all the uproar and the police coming and everything, I discovered that Kate had left me a message.

Well, I think it must have been Kate, and I think it must be a message, though it's a strange one. It's not a note – she hasn't written anything down. But when I pulled my duvet back to get into bed I found one of the pebbles from her collection, tucked underneath my pillow. I picked it up and turned it over in my hands; I thought she might have written something on it. But it was smooth and cool and completely blank. Just a pretty pebble.

My first thought was, *How did it get there?* Kate had left before me so how had she been in my room without me knowing? But then I remembered I was in the kitchen when she left, so she could have done it on her way down the stairs.

My second thought was, *What was she trying to tell me?* The pebble was there on purpose, so it must mean *something*.

I went up to her room the next morning before the policewomen came back. It looked like she'd just popped out and was coming back any minute. She'd pulled up the bedcovers but she hadn't bothered to smooth them out, and there were half-empty mugs and a cereal bowl on the floor, with the usual scattering of clothes. It made me feel awful to see it all and not see her.

The rest of Kate's pebble collection was still on a shelf. She'd chosen the biggest one to put in my room, but I didn't know if that meant anything.

A voice in my head said, *You mightn't ever be able to ask her that*, but I pushed it away.

Of course I'd ask her.

Of course I'd find her.

I wasn't *ever* going to give up.

I had to talk to Mum and Dad together. I was sick of hearing separate bits and pieces that didn't tie together or make any sense. I wanted them in the same place.

'You *have* to tell me what's been going on,' I said. 'I don't care if it's a secret, it's too late to keep a secret. And I don't care if you think it'll upset me because whatever it is, I can tell you that *not* knowing is a lot worse than knowing could ever be.'

We were all down in the basement kitchen, which seemed like another planet. For a start none of us could have eaten cakes, even if there'd been any. But Mum hadn't baked since Kate had disappeared; she was too worried to work. Her friend had taken over the whole job for a while, so the basement smelled of cleaning products instead of warm cakes.

And no one in our house was hungry, anyway. We pushed food around our plates at mealtimes, but we couldn't eat much. Mum even bought junk food to cheer us up, so there were bowls of crisps and sweets lying around. I still didn't feel hungry, though.

Mum put her arm round me.

'You're absolutely right, Mini darling,' she said. 'It's about time to be honest.'

Then she nodded at Dad, meaning that he should start. He thought for a moment, like he was working out where to begin.

'You know I was adopted, don't you, Mini?'

I nodded; of course I did. I'd always known that.

'And you know I had a bad time of it? With my adoptive parents, when they told me?'

I nodded again. I remember how he'd explained that being told he was adopted had all gone wrong. He said it had hit him like a sledgehammer, like his whole world had collapsed.

'You thought no one wanted you,' I said.

'Everyone's different,' Dad continued. 'Not everyone who's adopted feels bad about it – not by any means. Most people these days, they're told right from the start and it's fine. And lots of adopted people feel different in a *good* way – they've been chosen by the parents who adopted them, which is more than you can say if you're born to the parents you already have. You can't say we chose you, Sweet Pea, you just arrived!'

He smiled at me then, but the smile didn't reach his eyes. None of us had smiled properly since Kate had disappeared, and I wondered if we'd feel like doing big happy ones ever again.

Dad glanced at Mum before he went on. I could see he'd have loved to have had a cup or a plate to fiddle with. He was finding it hard, and I had to wonder if holding a big spoon would make it easier for him, like they did at Satch's house.

'Anyway, it was never like that for me,' he went on. 'I didn't feel chosen, and I took it hard. I don't blame my adoptive parents, they did what they thought was right, but it had a bad effect on me.'

I reached out and patted his hand, he looked so sad.

'You have to be told,' Dad said, and I suddenly wondered if he meant me, now, or him, back then. Maybe both?

'No question about that,' he continued. 'But the how, and the why, and how you feel about it, and what happens next...' Dad shifted in his seat, looked longingly at the row of empty cake boxes on the bench, and then turned back to me. 'I felt like the bottom had fallen out of my world, I can tell you. It took me ages to get back on my feet.'

I was starting to feel confused. I was still waiting to hear about Kate, and I couldn't see where Dad was going with this. Mum felt me shift impatiently, and she gave me a little squeeze and stroked my hair. But it all reminded me of how, last term, Ruby and her friends went on for weeks about being adopted. They ended up pretending they'd all been adopted and were actually lost princesses, which even they must have realised was unlikely.

Dad was *still* talking about his adoption.

'So,' he said, 'I never wanted that to happen to anyone I knew. No one I loved was going to feel like I had, if I could help it.'

Which Ruby and her gang would never appreciate, is what I was thinking to myself, when an enormous new idea hit me like a hurricane.

Kate.

Kate was adopted!

And suddenly, I knew that must be true.

I stared at Dad with what must have been the most shocked expression of the year, just as he was saying, 'Which was why things were so tricky with Kate.'

I think my jaw dropped, like with people in cartoons when they're surprised. I do know I couldn't say anything right then.

I even felt rooted to the spot, like they say in books when people are stunned with amazement. *Because how could I possibly have known?*

Mum took over the explaining.

'Kate was happy about it all. But later on – as she

grew up – she didn't want to know. Never wanted to talk about adoption, never wanted anyone else to know. So – well, because of how it had been for Peter – we didn't push it. We thought she'd come round to accepting it, sooner or later.'

I got my voice back.

'Why didn't either of you tell me before?'

There was a bit of a silence. Then Dad said, 'We were waiting for you to ask – like we waited for Kate to ask us.'

Oh, please. That has to be the stupidest idea yet. How could I ask, if I didn't know *what* to ask?

Dad might as well say, 'Well, Mini dear, you're really the Princess of Transpotamia, but you never asked us if you were, so of course, we never said.'

It's just ridiculous. The whole thing is as weird as anything could be, but there's something else that matters to me even more.

Why on earth didn't Kate ever tell me?

Mum said the reason they didn't insist on talking to Kate about it, was that she already knew.

'We fostered Kate when she was almost two, and then we started the adoption process about a year later: she was three and a half – almost four, in fact – when you arrived. I was expecting you when the papers came through – Kate's adoption papers – and you were born a month later.'

Dad looked at me with a little grin, and reached over and ruffled my hair.

'We started fostering because we thought we couldn't have babies of our own. And then you proved us wrong!'

'But you'd already adopted Kate?' I asked, glancing at both of them.

They both nodded.

'We knew we wanted to when we first saw her, when we were her foster parents,' Dad said. We hoped we could end up adopting her, and we did. And for her, well – you were the icing on the cake for Kate, you know. She fell for you the moment she first saw you. Just like we both did.'

I felt my eyes fill up with tears when he said that. I couldn't remember a time without Kate, and I couldn't remember a time when I hadn't loved her, either. And now that she'd run away I mightn't be able to tell her that again.

Not ever again.

Mum put both her arms round me, and Dad reached out and hugged us both. Mum and I were both crying and I think Dad was too; he certainly gave a big sniff.

'We'll find her, Mini,' he said into my hair. 'I promise you, we'll find her and bring her home.'

'But hang on,' I suddenly said, pulling away from them both. 'What about all the stuff with the tattoo and the papers? What was *that* about? I *still* don't know why she ran away!'

Mum handed me a tissue, but her face crumpled up again, and she looked at me in despair.

'It's such a mess,' she said. 'Kate's father – her birth father, I mean – wrote to us last month. We used to visit him when we were fostering Kate... Anyway, he wrote to tell us that Gwen – Kate's birth mother – had died.'

Mum got up from the bench, straightened the tea towels on the rack, which didn't need it, and then bent down to pick up an imaginary crumb off the floor.

'We hadn't heard from him in years,' she said, straightening up again. 'We'd lost touch. But he wanted to tell us that Gwen had died, and he sent something of hers for Kate.'

Mum pulled a face, the sort of expression you wear when you've got a stab of pain.

'And that's when the trouble started,' she said. 'That's when I made my big mistake.'

'*Our* mistake, Tiffany,' put in Dad. 'We *both* made it. Don't take all the blame yourself.'

Mum shot him a grateful glance, and I made another guess.

'You didn't tell Kate?'

Mum gave a little nod.

'Not right away. Kate found the letter before we'd had a chance to tell her about it,' she said.

'We were going to tell her – of *course* we were going to tell her,' said Dad quickly. 'We just hadn't decided how to, and your mum was so busy, and I wanted to think it through. Because Kate never – she always avoided talking about being adopted. So it was hard to see how to get it right...' His voice trailed off.

'So yes, sure, she was upset,' Mum said, starting up again. 'Anyone would be, finding something like that. Probably the worst bit for her was that she can't remember anything about her birth mother. Nothing at all.'

'And of course, she found the silver chain and butterfly pendant that he sent,' added Dad. 'Which somehow made it all worse.'

Another clue fell into place in my mind.

'But the very *idea* that we'd hidden it from her!' Mum said in despair. 'She knows better than that, she honestly does. All I did was stuff the envelope in the kitchen drawer until your dad and I had a chance to talk about it...'

'But she found it first,' I said, suddenly remembering the morning of Satch's cupcakes. 'And she got upset.'

'Well, yes,' agreed Mum. 'Anyone would, I know that, and I'm so, so sorry about it.' She gave a wobbly sigh.

'But getting a butterfly tattoo just to spite us? Saying terrible things? And then running off to heaven only knows where, without a word? It's – well, I can see how she must feel, but it's very hard on us. All of us.'

Mum turned to look at me.

'We don't have a clue where she's gone, Mini,' she said. 'Not to her birth father – that's the first place the police looked and she hasn't turned up. Anyway, I don't think Kate knows where he is. He didn't put his address on the letter.'

'Why did they give her away?' I asked. And then, like a weird echo in my head, I heard Kate's angry voice shouting at Mum the night she ran off to stay with Lee.

Why don't you give me back?

Oh, poor Kate.

Mum tried to explain it to me.

'Gwen – Kate's birth mother? – oh, maybe she was a bit wild. Or maybe she was just very young and not ready for the responsibility of being tied down with a baby. She probably hadn't realised what it would be like, looking after one.'

Mum glanced at me.

'It's not easy, you know,' she said. 'It's lovely, no question, but it's hard work. You have to want to do it and not mind about the mess, and having your life taken over. It was a bit of a shock for me when I started...' and she smiled, remembering.

Mum hates mess. She loves us, I know she does, but she has a lot of trouble with the mess we make.

'Anyway, Gwen left when Kate was just a baby,' she went on. 'Her father couldn't cope all by himself, and that's why Kate went into foster care. We used to take Kate to see him – even after you were little, for a while. But it faded out eventually – he couldn't really keep it going, however much he wanted to.' Then Mum looked up at me. 'Do you remember when we all went to meet him at that beach?'

The beach that Kate talked about!

Of course.

I could slot more bits of the jigsaw into place, but none of them told me how to find her. Not yet.

10

Days went by, and still there was no news.

Everyone tried to help us cope with missing Kate. Mum and Dad's friends turned up every day to do what they could. Even the neighbours we didn't like left a tuna casserole on our front steps.

Kate's friends came round to talk to Mum, which was nice of them. They came in two and threes to spin out the comfort, and they stayed to talk, it wasn't just hello and goodbye. They kept saying they were sure Kate was OK, even though I didn't believe they were sure of anything. No one could be.

After the first time they came around I looked for Mum, to see how she'd taken it. I found her in Kate's room, making the bed. She'd picked up the mugs and the cereal bowl and tidied up a bit, but it still looked like Kate had only popped out for a while. Which I hoped was true.

Mum stood in the middle of the room with a

cloth in her hand, and looked around.

'I don't know what else to do' she said softly. 'I don't want to tidy up too much, because I'd rather it looked like it usually does. But if I leave it messy, it could seem as though I don't care.'

She stood frowning for a moment and then she sighed, and her shoulders sort of sagged.

'It's so hard to get things right,' she said in a small voice, and gave me a shaky little smile just before her face crumpled up in tears. So we sat on the bed and cried some more, and I couldn't help wondering how much you can cry before you run out of tears.

Dad made posters with Kate's photo on them. He was sticking them up all over town, and planning to hand out leaflets on the street, and at the bus station. All his friends were helping.

I didn't go to school for the first few days. Mum and Dad said I should go back, because I'd be distracted and that would be helpful. But I couldn't bear to try to act normally. It felt like pretending nothing had happened, when it had.

Satch came round to see me on the second day. I think his mum might have phoned my mum first, but anyway he knew what had happened, the bare bones of it. I told him all about it, everything I knew, anyway. Like I said before, he's easy to tell things to. Also, I couldn't think about anything else, so no way could I *not* tell him.

I even told Satch how miserable I was that Kate had never told me she was adopted. I could tell he understood, and that was a comfort because I hadn't mentioned it to Mum or Dad. I thought it would make them even more unhappy than they already were, which didn't seem fair.

But Satch said, 'It sounds like Kate didn't even want to *think* about it, let alone talk. I don't reckon it was about telling *you*. She didn't want *anyone* to know. Most probably, she didn't want to know it herself.'

Then I told Satch about the pebble Kate had left for me. I wanted to talk about it, but not to Mum or Dad, because how could it help them? And that made Satch the ideal choice. He was interested, but he couldn't think of a reason any more than I could. He did say could it be just a last minute present from her because of me and geography, but I didn't agree.

'For one thing, the pebble's geology, not geography,' I pointed out to him. 'And it's not a present. If it was a present it would be a rubbish one, and Kate doesn't give rubbish presents. No, it's a sign. I *know* it's some sort of a sign, or a clue. She wants me to find her...'

'I know!' I suddenly had a crazy idea. Crazy, yes,

but still worth a try.

I jumped to my feet.

'Wait here!'

Satch and I were downstairs in the den. I ran up to my room, got the pebble, and tore down again. Then I shut the den door behind me for a bit of privacy, pulled the swivel chair out from the desk, and sat down in it, holding the pebble in front of me. Satch just stared, and then grinned in amusement. Naturally, he didn't have a clue what I was on about.

'Oh, hang on!'

I'd forgotten something. I dropped the pebble on the floor.

'The compass! We need a compass!'

I ran upstairs again and found my best compass, ran back, and gave the compass to Satch. Then I sat down in the chair, held the pebble in my lap, closed my eyes tight, and told Satch to spin the chair. I didn't explain what I was doing until later, and at the time he probably thought I'd gone mad, but he did it anyway.

You'll probably guess what was in my mind.

If Dad was right about me having extra iron in my nose for finding directions, maybe I could use the iron to find Kate? If I concentrated hard on her while the chair was spinning, maybe the chair would end up pointing to where Kate had gone?

It didn't work, though. I did say I thought it was crazy.

Satch spun the chair four times, and each time I concentrated so hard on Kate I thought my head would explode. But the chair stopped with me pointing in a different direction every time, and none of the directions seemed to say *Kate* to me, anyway.

I was disappointed, though. Oh, I knew it was silly, but at least it was an *idea*. I was short of good ones and now I was even shorter of them. What else could I try?

I pushed the chair back to the desk and dropped the pebble on the floor, but this time I accidentally trod on it. It hurt a lot.

I said a word I don't often use and Satch looked surprised, but I felt so frustrated with everything. The pebble; the compass; the chair; Satch. And most of all, with Kate. But the next moment everything changed.

Because when I bent down to scoop the pebble off the floor I didn't pick it up after all. I just stayed crouched down, staring at it.

There was complete silence in the den for a minute. Then Satch coughed a sort of, *Excuse me! What is going on now?* cough. I knew he must think I'd lost my mind, crouched over a pebble on the floor. But I was thinking so hard I didn't pay him any attention for a minute.

Then I said, 'It's not just a pebble.'

There was another silence.

Satch said, 'What?'

'It's not a pebble,' I repeated, sitting down on the floor and picking it up carefully.

Satch walked across and looked down. Then, like he had with the cupcakes, he just sort of *looked* a question at me.

I grinned at him. Suddenly I felt light, as if a great big weight had fallen away from me. Or like I had found a way to wind back time and stop an earthquake from happening.

'It's not a pebble,' I repeated. 'It's a stone.'

Satch raised his eyebrows higher.

'It's a stone, like the ones the Stone Tower's made of,' I added.

Satch stared at me. It was like he'd realised he was talking to a certified alien from a parallel universe, and didn't know what to do about it.

'You lost me, Mini,' he said finally. 'About five minutes ago.'

I tried to explain. About the travel game and about how we were going to start a new journey from the Silk Road to look for the Stone Tower. And how Kate had gone on about wanting to travel over sand, and about a beach holiday we'd had when we were little.

'And Mum mentioned the same beach holiday to me, the other day. She said we'd all gone to meet Kate's father there – her birth father, I mean,' I corrected myself.

Satch frowned.

'So, you think Kate's telling you about that beach, by leaving you the stone?'

I nodded happily.

'Yup! That's what I think. I reckon she's saying, *I've gone to the beach.*

Satch folded himself down on to the floor beside me, a bit like the way giraffes do in TV nature programmes.

'But she might just be saying, um, *Don't worry, Mini. I'll be back soon, and then we can go on the Stone Tower journey,* he pointed out.

I thought about that. He could be right.

And then I had a better idea.

'Photos!' I said. 'I bet there are photos of the holiday. Of the beach, even.'

I kind of remembered that there were some photos I hadn't seen for years. I could look on the den shelves for them; we keep albums and boxes of photos there.

And then I realised something else...

That man – I sat on his shoulders at the beach, and the other day I'd thought it was Dad.

But it wasn't Dad at all. It must have been Kate's father.

How utterly and completely weird it was that I never knew that before.

It was easier to find the old photo albums than I'd expected, because they were all on the first shelf. Afterwards, I wondered if Mum – or even Kate – had been looking at them recently.

'Come on, look for a beach!' I said. I gave one album to Satch and took another one myself.

We'd got through five old albums of me and Kate at the park, and our first days at school, and birthday parties and nativity plays and all that, before I found the right one.

There were only three photos on a beach, but it was the same beach in all of them. I thought it must be The Beach, not just any old beach. No one had talked about other beach holidays and I don't remember any, not that I'd be a good witness. I don't remember much from way back then; I was too small.

The edge of a far-away memory tugged at my mind when I studied the photos. Three grown-ups and two little children, on a big sandy beach, with the tide out.

Not much of a clue, I thought at first.

The baby must be me. I can't say I recognised myself, because I was all wrapped up with a little hat on, and my face didn't show. Still, it must be, the one holding a whirly windmill thing, because the other girl, the older one, is absolutely Kate. Holding my hand in two of the photos and looking very serious in all of them. Just like I remember her from way back then.

And definitely Dad, too, standing with another man who had to be Kate's birth father. He was looking down at her, so you can't see his face. He looked – oh, I don't know.

Tall. Thin. Not very much like Kate.

Mum isn't in that picture, so I suppose she must have been the one who took it. It was just a photo of the people and the beach; you can't see much else. But in the next one I could see the background more clearly. Mum and Dad are both in that one with us, and he – Kate's birth father – isn't, so he must have taken it.

I passed it to Satch.

'Look – what's that? Behind me and Kate? On the edge of the sand?'

I already knew what it was, but I wanted him to say it first.

Satch stared at the photo, and then looked at me. He grinned, and did a sort of one-handed salute.

'It's your tower, Mini,' he said, handing the album back.

A round stone tower. Not all that big – just a lot bigger than the people in the photo. Not as big as a lighthouse, say – sort of shorter, and squat. And made from stones, because you can see some of them showing through where the walls had started to crumble.

The Stone Tower!

It *had* to be right. I just knew it was.

But I still needed to know *where* it was, and I didn't have the faintest clue about that. Mum hadn't said where the beach was, and the album wasn't the sort where you write captions; it was the kind where you slip photos behind sheets of see-through filmy stuff. But then Satch had the idea of taking the photos out from behind the film, and flipping them over.

And there, in Mum's writing on all three of them, it said: On the beach at Dympton. I read it out loud.

'I know where Dympton is,' said Satch, looking up. 'Our Uncle Ted used to live there.'

So then I worked out with Satch what I knew, and what I still didn't know. It was like when I planned out the earthquake project, being all organised and efficient about putting the facts in the right order. It's actually rather soothing; I can recommend it.

First, we worked out what I was sure about.

I was certain that the beach in the photos was The Beach, like the tower was The Tower. And I knew that Kate had left me a clue about it.

But what I didn't know was what the clue actually meant.

Either she was saying, *Look Mini, I'm all right, don't worry, I've only gone back to the beach.*

Or else she was saying, *Look, Mini, this is where I am, come and find me.*

I talked it back and forth with Satch, and in the end I decided that I'd go after her anyway. Because whatever she meant, I knew she needed my help. So I wanted to find her, and be there for her like she'd always been there for me.

And bring her home again, if I could.

11

Satch offered to come with me, but I decided that I'd go by myself. I didn't want to risk getting Satch into trouble, and I knew there was bound to be some for me, because I wasn't going to tell Mum and Dad what I was doing.

Satch helped me work out how to get there – not that it was hard, and to be honest I didn't exactly need help because it's what I'm good at. But still, it was nice of him. There were two train journeys and one bus, and the timetables were all on the Internet. I could get to Dympton in about two and a half hours; probably less if I started early and if the connections worked out.

So if I said I was going back to school the next morning but caught the train instead, Mum and Dad needn't know until much later.

Satch frowned, and shook his head. That was the bit that worried him – that I was going without telling them. If I'm honest, it worried me too.

But what else could I do? Kate had left the clue for me, and I knew that she was upset with both of them, but not with me. So telling them, and maybe having them come with me – well, I didn't think it would work. If Kate saw Mum and Dad she might just run away again, even further this time. Then there'd be no chance of finding her.

And what if I was wrong? What if she wasn't there at all? They'd have got their hopes up for nothing.

So I decided to go into school first thing for registration, and leave after that. Satch said he'd try to cover for me the rest of the day, even though he wasn't happy about it.

It was the best I could do.

Satch was waiting for me at school the next morning.

'Take my mobile,' he offered. 'Then you can call home, if you need to. Ask for help, even.' He lent me money, too, because I didn't have much – enough for the fares and a bit more, but not enough for unexpected extras.

I packed all that away, but he was still holding out a carrier bag. He just smiled in silence, like I had with the box of Mum's cupcakes when we first met.

This time it was me not saying anything – I just took the bag and opened it. Inside there was a lunch box, and an iPod.

'I thought you might need something to eat,' Satch said in a casual way. I didn't realise he'd actually *made* the sandwiches until I opened the box on the train.

'And you're lending me your iPod?' I said, inspecting it. I was impressed.

'It's only an old one,' Satch said quickly. 'Tom gave it to me when he got a better one. And you mightn't like my music,' he added. 'I dunno what you like. But still...' The T sounds were tripping him up, so I knew he was nervous.

'Sure I will!' I felt seriously gratified. It sort of cemented our friendship, in a way.

'It might be too much jazz,' he added. I just stared at him blankly.

'Or maybe too much Louis Armstrong,' he added. 'Though you *have* to like him, everyone's got to like him. He's the absolute best.'

'Oh...OK,' I said. I'd never heard of him.

'But not everyone knows what Louis Armstrong's nickname was,' said Satch, grinning at me. He was enjoying this, I could tell, because he knew I didn't have a clue what he was on about.

'No, I don't either,' I agreed, waiting to hear what

he was getting to.

'It was Satchmo'.'

I just said 'Oh,' without thinking. Then I realised what he'd said, and did a double take.

'*Oh*!' I said again. '*That's* why, is it?'

'Yeah, that's it,' he said with a grin. 'I can't get on with my real name,' he added. 'I gave it up years ago. Satch'll do me fine.'

I looked at him thoughtfully, and then I raised my eyebrows in a silent question. Satch paused for a moment, looking doubtful, and glanced around. But then he nodded.

'Will you go first?' I felt weird about telling him.

'What about we do it together?' Satch suggested. Maybe he felt weird as well.

'At the same time, you mean? Out loud?' I wanted to be sure.

He nodded, and glanced around again. 'But keep the volume down, eh?'

'One, two, three!'

So then we leant in towards each other, which meant I had to stand on my toes to get close to his ear. And we said our real and embarrassing names out loud to each other, in as close to a whisper as we could manage.

Is Clive *really* such a terrible name?

I don't think so. I think I can be confident I'll still

151

win the embarrassment medal.

I ate Satch's sandwiches on the second train ride. Sim had drawn a label for them with a picture of Satch on it, and *The World's Best Sandwich Man* written underneath with a rainbow pencil. He might be right, too. There was hummus and chopped dates on one layer, and banana on raisin bread on the other one. Dad, the other sandwich king in my life, would be impressed, and so was I.

Then I listened to some of Satch's music, but I definitely preferred the sandwiches. I have since discovered that jazz can mean a lot of different things, and I liked the Louis Armstrong bits, but some of the other playlists were too squeaky-squawky for me.

I still want an iPod, though.

The bus journey was much quicker than the trains, and then I just walked from where the bus stopped in Dympton, right down to the beach.

I sort of remembered it when I saw it.

I hadn't even thought to worry where to look for Kate, or what I'd do if I couldn't find her, but she was there all right – I spotted her as soon as I looked around. She was sitting on the beach, leaning against the Stone Tower with her backpack on the sand beside her. She looked pretty scruffy; I wondered if she'd been sleeping rough.

She must have heard me coming but she didn't move or look around, she just kept staring out across the beach to the sea. I plumped myself down beside her and looked at her, and then I reached over and patted her knee. I suddenly felt like I was the older sister and she was the one who needing looking after.

'I've come to take you home,' I said. She still didn't look at me, though; she just kept looking out to sea.

I tried again.

'I've never had a birthday without you,' I said. 'I don't want to start now, Kate. You have to come home.'

'I've had birthdays without you, though,' she said. Her voice sounded creaky, like she hadn't been talking much, or maybe she'd been crying a lot. 'But I don't remember them,' she went on. 'I don't remember anything about them. I wish I did, and I don't. I thought coming here would help sort my head out, and it hasn't.'

I put my hand on her shoulder, and patted her a bit more. She didn't seem to notice but on the other hand, she didn't pull away.

'It's like when you come in to a movie after it's started,' she added. 'You know? You've missed the first bit and you have to catch up later on.'

She turned and looked at me then, and I nodded to encourage her.

'I've missed the first bit of my life,' she said. Her voice broke and went all husky, but she kept talking. 'And now I've lost my chance for ever – and I *still* don't think Mum and Dad have a clue what I'm on about.'

I wasn't sure that I did, either, but I was trying.

'Here's the thing, though,' I suggested. 'I know now what happened, about your birth mother dying, and you finding out, all that.'

It was very hard not to add: *And why didn't you ever tell me?* But I didn't, not then. I knew I had to wait.

'But Kate – Mum and Dad, *they're* your Mum and Dad!'

She didn't say anything and she was looking out to sea again, but I knew she was listening.

'They've *always* been your Mum and Dad,' I said firmly. 'Ever since they first saw you.'

I sat there, willing her to agree, but she didn't answer. She didn't say anything at all.

'Don't you think so?' I asked. She still didn't reply.

'Look Kate,' I said. 'If you don't think so – if they're *not* your Mum and Dad – then I'm not your sister!'

My eyes suddenly flooded with tears. I hadn't thought it might all still go wrong, but now I knew it could. That she might just – just ignore me. Give up on me.

'I need you, Kate!' I said, desperately. 'Please don't do this to me...' My voice went wobbly and I couldn't finish, but Kate suddenly reached out her hand and grabbed mine. We sat there, not even looking at each other, just holding on tight. Like we were little kids lining up for class with our best friends.

There was more silence, but not such a bad one.

'And they love you,' I said firmly, squeezing her hand. Kate did a sort of snort – a *harrumph!* noise.

'Yes, they do,' I said. I was getting back into my stride now. 'Listen to me. The other night, Mum said she wouldn't change a single thing about you. Not a hair on your head and not a drop of the ink on your tattoo.'

Kate looked at me doubtfully, and raised one eyebrow.

I grinned.

'Yeah, well, OK – she didn't say that second thing. But I bet she would if she'd thought of it – if she thought it would help. She loves you, Kate. They both do. They'd do anything to put it right again.'

I bet they'll even sit around the table with us, taking

turns to hold the talking spoon, is what I thought.

There was more silence then, but I didn't say anything else. We just sat together, looking out across the beach at the sea, still holding hands.

After a while the sun went in and it got a bit chilly, so we walked back along the beach front to the cafe. I was glad of Satch's money because Kate had almost run out of hers. I had fish and chips and Kate had a veggie burger and chips, and we ate them in silence. I felt better, partly because of the food but mostly because I thought it was actually going to work.

And I let the silence keep going, like I had learned to do. I just waited for Kate to speak, and I didn't even need to make up a list in my head while I was waiting. And she did start talking, in the end.

'I hated it when they didn't tell me my birth father had sent that letter. And my butterfly chain.'

I would have hated it too. I nodded at her.

'It was such a shock to me, Mini. My mum who had me, my birth mother, dying and me not even knowing. And reading it in a letter *not even to me*, from my – my other dad. And it felt like a lie. I'm frightened of lies,' she went on. 'It was – it was like I was an apple, and someone bit a massive chunk out of me.' She paused again.

'I still feel like that,' she added softly.

'They were *going* to tell you,' I said cautiously.

156

'Truly. They didn't get it right, but they know that. They *know* they screwed up. But I honestly think they'll try harder now.'

I really did understand how she felt. Because maybe not saying something – something that's really important – can be a sort of a lie? And this is not the same thing, but Dad only told me two nights ago the real reason why they named me what they did, which I might as well say now, since I've told Satch.

It's Ermintrude.

It was Dad's birth mother's name.

I ask you.

I'm never going to use it. I think Dad accepts that now.

'I got seriously overwhelmed by it all,' Kate finally said, dipping her last chip into a puddle of tomato sauce. 'I didn't know how to stop being angry and feeling hurt. So I started tormenting Mum and Dad to show them I'd found out. Trying to make them talk to me, or something. And I don't know…I just kept on going along the overwhelmed route, and I got deeper and deeper.'

She put her finger into the sauce and then licked her finger, exactly like Dad does when he thinks no one's looking. I still find it hard to believe she's not his birth daughter.

I couldn't help remembering what Mum had said, about how you can start off down a road and forget the way home.

'You couldn't find a way to get underwhelmed,' I suggested.

'Not even just whelmed,' she agreed, with the ghost of a smile.

After lunch we went back on the beach, and walked along to the Stone Tower. Kate patted its curving side affectionately.

'See, Mini?' she said. 'I've found it now! We don't need to go looking for it when we grow up, after all.'

'No orchards near here, though,' I pointed out. 'I'd still like to look for the real one someday.'

Which I would.

Then I took a deep breath.

'Never mind about that now,' I said. 'You have to come home with me, Kate, you really do. It's my birthday *next week*. And like I said, I couldn't have a birthday without you being there.'

Kate looked at me. I grabbed her hand again.

'And I am *so* sick of being twelve,' I added. 'So help me, Kate! *I have to have this birthday!*'

Kate looked like she might almost smile at any moment. I thought I had probably won, with any luck. But I still couldn't be sure.

Then she put her arms round me and hugged me fiercely.

'No more secrets, Mini, I promise. Not from you.'

'No more lies, either. We'll have a new family rule about it,' I agreed.

'Yeah, right. We'll put it on the wall planner!'

Kate sighed. If a sigh can wobble, hers did.

'Why do I have to find stuff out the hard way?' she asked.

'But you don't usually do that,' I pointed out. 'That's more like me than you. Satch says I start off going at things the hard way, so every little problem gets right up my nose. But you don't. Or, anyway, you didn't used to – that's not your real nature.'

'What is my real nature, Mini?' Kate looked at me intently. I smiled encouragingly at her.

'It must be a kind one,' I said. 'You're coming back home with me even when you're not sure you want to – *just because you don't want to spoil my birthday.*'

Kate stared at me for a long moment while I held my breath. Then she smiled back. It was a wobbly smile, but definitely a smile.

'OK,' she agreed. 'But can we go on the camels?'

I nodded.

'There's no better way to travel,' I said. 'Especially over sand.'